THEY DIDN'T KNOW WHAT TO SAY

Half Inch Press

Other books by Beate Sigriddaughter

Fiction
The New Parcival
The Unicorn And...
Snow White: A Mirror in Several Voices
Beauty Sleeping
Audrey: A Book of Love
Dona Nobis Pacem
Soleil Madera

Poetry
A Well-Behaved Skeptic
Letters to a Stranger
Xanthippe and Her Friends
Dancing in Santa Fe and other poems
Emily
Kaleidoscope
Wild Flowers
Circus Dancer

Aphorisms
Kuan Yin: Flowers for Change
Postcards to a Young Unicorn

THEY DIDN'T KNOW WHAT TO SAY

BEATE SIGRIDDAUGHTER

Table of Contents

Women and Men

I Didn't Know What to Say

I didn't know what to say. That's how it started.

I still don't know what to say. We're sitting in the kitchen. I can't believe I am sitting here, hating the man across the table. It isn't his fault, but I have to hate someone. And he's on hand. Why did he have to bring her here? Why did they have to visit? The smell of the tomatoes growing in the planters just outside the kitchen door is making me sick and it's not early pregnancy sick either. This is eighth month heaviness, and it's hot and I feel huge. Sweat trickling down the side of my neck. Also down my cleavage. I feel like an elephant. His name is Derek, and I keep reminding myself it isn't his fault. He doesn't know what to say either. Is he feeling sorry for me?

"Do you want a beer?" I ask. "Or water? I think there's some iced tea as well." I marvel how I can even come up with coherent words.

"No thanks," he says, lifting his glass which contains something the color of beer or iced tea to show me he's good as far as liquids are concerned. Good, because I don't want to get up.

His eyes are kind, dark brown with flecks of gold, and lots of crow's feet. The baby is kicking, slowly, lazily. It is hot, and I don't want to move at all. Otherwise, I'd be gone. To the bedroom. To lie down. Better yet, to pack a suitcase. Call a cab to take me to the Greyhound station. Where would I go?

She's beautiful, his Christina. Well, not his exactly. They're not married. Not like me and Matt. They're just traveling together for the summer. He's lucky to have her I suppose. Except today. Today Matt is the lucky one. I can't believe it. I don't want to believe it. Yes, yes, it was no secret that Matt and Christina were lovers once upon a time. That's not the problem here. Once upon a time is one thing. But when they went off together to the guest house, which we call the gazebo, but it's really a house with walls and air conditioning and white lace curtains that I made and hung up just three weeks ago, and a bathroom with toilet and shower, I was paralyzed.

"For old times' sake," Matt said as though asking for our blessing. Christina merely smiled.

And I didn't know what to say.

Derek didn't say anything either, just looked intrigued and a bit embarrassed. And then they walked out, side by side, leaving us here at the kitchen table. They didn't touch on the way to the guest house. Plenty of time for touching now that they are out of sight.

I should have said no. My whole being was screaming no. No. No. No. Derek should have said no. It is too late. For old times' sake. I feel so heavy, so humiliated.

I watch Derek peel an apple from the bowl in the middle of the table and cut it into segments. That must be his own pocketknife. I don't recognize it. Now he is pushing the plate my way. I have no appetite. I feel humiliated. And hot. He must think all this so bizarre. He must think of me as such a doormat.

If I have a miscarriage, I will leave Matt. If Emily is born, I don't know what I will do. I won't have a miscarriage of course. I am healthy. Robust. I want to raise her as a strong woman. How can I ever look at Matt again without shame, that he was capable of risking everything for one moment of for old times' sake? How can I ever forgive him? For apparently not even having a clue that what he is doing is wrong?

If only I had something to keep my hands busy. Embroidery, like the ladies had in ancient times.

I see myself in a light blue beaded dress, impossibly beautiful, with my daughter in my arms at the steps to a castle or a church or a cave. Alone. I don't see Matt with us. Should I have known it would be like this when I married Matt? Were there signs I ignored? Is he the stupid one? Am I? Will I ever be able to look into his eyes again without feeling shock or shame?

So much regret. And in the end, I will accuse myself that it is all my fault. Because I didn't know what to say. Because I wasn't compelling enough to make him not even think of old times.

Derek stands up and takes the three steps to the window. Should I offer to show him the garden? Act as though everything is normal? Give us something to do? I won't. I don't even want to get up.

He looks at the bird feeder over the tomatoes. A towhee, a house finch, a few yellow-bellied finches. He is very tall. Does he think this is normal? People just casually wandering off to make love for old times' sake?

She stirs again, not a kick, just a flutter. My daughter. I will do anything to protect you. I will make you grow into a lioness, not a mouse. Not like me. Maybe that's what I'll call you. Not Emily. Leona. Lion girl.

So many dreams are dimming now.

Surprise Visit

She didn't know how to drive, so he picked her up at the Greyhound station at 1:20 a.m. It brought back bittersweet memories. Years ago, he had taken Melinda to another bus station in another town after a bustling ecumenical youth conference in Collegeville where his father had been one of the seminar facilitators. He'd been a junior in college, she a high school senior. While they both had attended all the lectures and discussions, they had also spent long hours of two consecutive nights kissing as though their lives depended on it. Now they were married but living in different cities because different graduate schools had offered them scholarships. She lived in a group house in Albuquerque with another woman and three guys, while he had an efficiency near the university in Las Cruces.

"What's wrong?" he asked her when she tumbled out of the bus in her jeans and sweater and the usual dark brown clogs, grimy and haggard looking. Though given the hour, that was hardly a surprise.

"Wrong? No, nothing is wrong. I just wanted to see you."

It's what she had said on the telephone earlier. She hadn't convinced him. They were long past the stage of initial infatuation when merely wanting to see him might have been an overwhelming and undeniable desire. At this stage in their lives, their respective scholarship stipends weren't so generous that the cost of an impromptu weekend roundtrip wouldn't have made a serious dent in their budgets, and budget considerations often trumped mere desire. They usually saw each other once a month or so, and he'd just been up to Albuquerque and was planning to go again two weeks from now.

"You're tired," he said. "Let's get you home and to bed. I'm tired too."

Late in the morning, almost noon when she finally

stirred awake, he started stroking her hair. It had never been an official signal for sex between them, but often enough it had worked like a question mark. If she wanted more, she would then turn to him and kiss him. She didn't. Instead, she moved out of his reach, turned away from him and swung her legs over the edge of the bed and sat still for a moment. So much for just wanting to see him. He placed his hand on her right shoulder. She didn't move any further away but didn't otherwise respond to his touch.

"Something is wrong," he said.

"Not really."

His mind spun around possible scenarios. She'd had sex with another guy and felt guilty. No, not likely. That wasn't like her at all. Guilt over something, perhaps. But sex, no. She hadn't smelled of sex either when she stepped off the bus, but then again, she had boarded late at night with plenty of time to clean up between her frenetic afternoon call and getting on the bus at nine or ten or whenever it was. From his end, he had to cut short a dinner with a fellow graduate student. An attractive female graduate student at that. He hadn't really wanted Melinda to come all that way on a whim and had tried to dissuade her.

"I'll be up in two weeks to see you anyway."

Her answer had been, "I want to see you now. Today. Or, well, early tomorrow morning anyway."

So, he had cut his dinner short. It had been awkward. "I need to pick up my wife at the bus station at the ungodly hour of 1:00 a.m. or thereabouts."

There was something almost gratifying in his fellow student's response. "Oh, I didn't know you had a wife."

"Sometimes I wonder myself," he had quipped.

Now, looking at Melinda's hunched back, he regretted having said something so flippant. Even though she would never know.

He spent the better part of Sunday trying to tease out what was going on. With little success. He asked about her recent exams, which she had aced, her thesis, which was coming along just fine, and her roommates, where her response came after a tiny pause, but then she reassured him they were all okay. The only thing that elicited a peal of laughter from her was when he asked her if she was pregnant. She wasn't, which was a relief, for children weren't in the grand plan for the next few years.

He meandered through his Sunday New York Times which, for him, was akin to going to church. They took a walk in Mesilla Valley Bosque State Park. He felt a great need to protect her, to shelter her. But he couldn't address whatever she obviously didn't want to address. The closest she came to revealing any kind of unease was when she mentioned Friday night's party at her group house.

"I was drinking too much," she said.

"And?"

"And nothing."

"Did something happen?"

"No."

"Well, whatever didn't happen, I'm here for you."

He insisted on driving her back to Albuquerque after dinner. She had a return trip ticket, but he persuaded her to never mind that. She'd have to take a bus before 5 o'clock in the morning, and he'd have to take her to the bus station anyway. Finally, she accepted. He felt an acute sense of disconnect from her all during the drive. Shortly before Socorro she fell asleep and slept almost all the rest of the way. It pleased him. It was something he could do for her, to give her a chance to sleep after what must have been as strange a day for her as it had been for him.

He stopped in her house to use the bathroom and say hello to one of her roommates who was watching TV in the common area living room.

"Be safe now," he said as he touched the door handle of his car. She had come back outside with him to see him off. It was cool at 11:00 p.m. She stood with her arms wrapped tightly around her.

"Okay," she said.

She looked as though he should stay with her or take her back with him. He almost said so. But there were appointments to keep, courses to teach, and two fierce independences to defend.

Lots of time to think on his way back to Las Cruces. How he should have pressed more. Asked outright maybe. It was the secrecy he found so disturbing. He trusted her. To a point. But that was just the thing. To a point. Too many things were unsaid between the two of them these days. And in a way he preferred it that way. He really didn't want to know her secret. Whatever it was, he was really not all that interested. Some parts of him had lately been wondering. Had he made a mistake? Whose idea was it anyway to get married? Truth was, it had been his. He proposed to her at the bottom of the second wooden ladder at Bandelier. She'd been pitching a fit about something or other and he'd stopped her, hugged her, and asked her to marry him. Everybody said they were way too young. Probably true. But he didn't want to lose her, not her long beautiful legs, her wide strong shoulders, her sharp, challenging mind. She was adorable and infuriating in equal measure. He would have to teach her how to drive and then find a way of financing an additional car. He hoped her ordeal, her unspoken reason for needing to be with him for what turned out a mere twenty-two hours, wasn't something unbearably horrible. He wondered if they would stay together for life. That had been the plan, of course. He missed their early days of infatuation when everything was simple. She probably missed that time too. She had seemed so transparent then, so open. Now it had all become excruciatingly complicated, and studying politics and history was way easier than successfully conducting a viable relationship with all its always shifting parts.

Not from the Neighbors

It wasn't ideal. Still, she felt lucky. Last winter he bought her a mink jacket. Sorry, environmentalists, but that had been her dream since she was a little girl and read about a movie star who wore an entire full length mink coat. And this summer they had planned to go to Santa Fe for the opera. *The Magic Flute*. It would have been spectacular. But then it got cancelled due to the virus. *Tristan and Isolde* would have been good, too, except it would have reminded her ever so painfully that she had never had an epic true love in her life. But *c'est la vie*. She had the house she wanted. Right on the beach. True, there was that easement that allowed other people's children to dash about on the beach and yell and carry on all day. But even in normal times, at night it was usually quiet, just the endless beautiful roar of the waves. And soon enough, when this virus thing was over, her own little boy would be cavorting on the beach with the others. Little Eric. She hoped he'd be a leader of the pack. She'd have to serve lemonade and sandwiches to his little friends, or granola bars, because they'd all want to come in to cool off on a hot afternoon. Not a problem. That's what Ellie was for, the *au pair* from London. Or whoever came after Ellie. Good thing Ellie had arrived before travel pretty much came to a stop. And good thing she didn't want to go home; she had decided to stay.

Tonight they were going out to dinner, she and Tom, first time since some of the restaurants had reopened. She was putting on eyeshadow and mascara for the first time in months. Her eyes were her best feature anyway and she wanted to make sure they would look good even with a mask underneath. Some crow's feet, yes, but they didn't look half bad. She had already put on her indigo silk dress. It fit perfectly. One of the few things that hadn't changed in recent weeks.

"Come in, come in," she sang at the knock at the

bathroom door.

Tom cautiously stuck in his head, then sidled the rest of the body through the door. She watched him through the mirror she still faced, painting on lip liner. Something was wrong. She could see it on his face. Didn't want to risk going out after all? She'd be okay with that. It made her a bit queasy, first time out after all this isolation.

"I, er... You look great," he said. His face in the mirror a study in misery.

"What is it?" she asked. He hadn't come in to deliver a compliment, though flattery was always welcome.

"You said you didn't want to hear it from the neighbors."

"Huh?"

"You said, you know...a little after Eric was born, that you didn't want to hear it from the neighbors. If I ever had an affair. Well. I sort of promised. So here goes. I'm having an affair."

"Ellie?" she asked. His face was flushed dark red in the mirror. Hers was a ghostly pale.

True, she had told him that. Bravado. Recklessness. Whatever. True, she didn't want to hear it from the neighbors. But she hadn't wanted this either.

The Mistress

Not what any of us expected, that's for sure.

I remember our first meeting. I was at Starbucks reading a magazine article about Frida Kahlo. It wasn't all that crowded. Nevertheless, she stopped at my table, something frothy in a mug in her hand.

"May I join you?"

"Sure," I said.

"I'm Linda. Linda Thomas."

"I know who you are."

"Oh."

Greg had pointed her out to me one day in the public library where we met at the circulation desk by chance. She was studying the bulletin board. Small, dark short curls, almost translucent porcelain skin. Ethereal somehow. He didn't call her over to introduce us. Lovely, I'd thought then with a quick pang of guilt. But not nearly as lovely as now when she was sitting across from me at Starbucks.

"I'm Melody." I extended my hand. She hesitated a fraction of a moment, then she reached across the table to shake.

"If you already know who I am, then you probably also know why I want to talk to you," she said.

"Yes. Greg."

"You're beautiful," she said breathily. "So I can understand."

I looked into her eyes, and I had goosebumps on my arms, on my ankles. I knew my life as I had known it would not be the same ever again. All of a sudden, we were in a lengthy and involved exchange of mutual admiration, which hasn't stopped to this day.

This day. She's moving in today. We haven't told him yet. That is to say, I haven't told him yet. I don't know how to do it. Somehow, I kept hoping he'd figure it out on his own. Instead, it's become my job to break the news. Well, okay, I did volunteer, though I regret that now. Seeing the discomfort in her eyes, though, what else could I do? Still, she'd be better qualified, no? She's known him longer. Better. Though I don't know about better. Thing is, he has to be told. Sooner or later. Preferably sooner. That's all there is to it.

He really was quite wonderful as a lover. Exciting. Uplifting. I had dreams of doing my precious artwork 24/7 with minimal interruptions because he'd be busy spending time with his wife and his career. No children, thank God. And from time to precious time, he'd be with me. He always brought me roses. We always made love. It always was delicious. But always amounted to once a week or every two weeks for a few hours. It didn't disturb my comfortable solitary life. I liked being part-time lover to a man committed to staying with his wife. It gave me this shining sense of being loved and noble both. Far be it from me to disrupt a marriage.

He told me right from the start he would never leave her. I readily bought into that, with just the tiniest ache in my heart, to be sure, especially when he'd keep harping on his commitment to her, but I still got to maintain my illusion of being noble. He told me he loved her. She was fragile and not sexually inclined. But lovely. Well, he was wrong. She's neither fragile nor asexual, though he was spot on about the lovely part. I'd never been with a woman before. Neither had she. We had no trouble figuring it out.

What we haven't figured out yet is how to let him know. We definitely don't want a threesome. As far as we know, he's still under the impression that she's moving out as a trial separation to sort things out for herself. For which reason he hasn't been with me for weeks now, a few months actually, because he felt he needed to sort things out on the home front, mending fences and all that. This of course made it convenient for me to avoid the issue which now can no longer be avoided. I did ask him once on the telephone, what if those fences can't be mended? He shrugged it off, confident that he could fix everything, given a chance. That in itself didn't come as a huge surprise. It was typical for him to interpret the world in his favor.

This might sound like a comedy, but it isn't funny. It might sound like poetic justice, but it isn't that either. Maybe it's all for the best. Per Linda, he likes novelty. And we like each other. She cried when she told me one time that once she's gone, he probably won't even notice, though his ego might. The tears were not so much over him, but over how negligible she felt in this world. I hope I can keep making her feel important.

As for me, I have no idea how my artwork will fare with all this imminent commotion. Unlike Linda, I haven't lived with another person since sharing a dormitory room first semester in college. And now, instead of painting flowers and mermaids, I'm hanging a glass bead curtain in what is to be her room. She really is lovely.

The Muse

He should never have talked to her. He should have taken a taxi anyway, but it felt like one of his last chances of slumming it. He was on the shuttle to Dulles Airport about to fly to an audition with the music director of the Los Angeles Symphony. At this point, it was just a formality. Even if he blew it, he was in. Still, that's what he should have focused on. But there she was, blond, with enormous blue eyes, in animated conversation with her seat neighbor, a much larger woman with an enormous bosom. Also blond. But it was the littler one in the aisle seat that fascinated him. She had a lovely melodic voice. Some kind of accent he couldn't place. Almost like a Scandinavian lilt, but not quite that. At times she leaned into her big-bosomed neighbor's shoulder, laughing. Something in him shifted. He willed her to turn to look at him. She never did.

Then it happened that he stood right behind them as they were about to get in the long snaking line for their security check. Soon enough he'd be boarding with first class and might not need to go through quite that long a line ever again.

"Where are you two ladies headed?"

"She is going to L.A.," the little one responded with a dazzling smile. Her friend didn't acknowledge him.

"Oh, so am I. And you?" He tried to hold his violin case so that she couldn't miss it. He wanted her to know he was important, not just any old schmuck captivated by her.

"I just came along on the shuttle to see her off."

They were approaching the person checking tickets or boarding passes, and the little one gave her friend a farewell hug and stepped to the side. He presented his ticket, got in line, then quickly turned around and stepped out of line again to where she still stood.

"Er," he said. "I'd love to talk to you when I get back. Here's my card. Will you give me a call? And soon? Next week maybe? Because I'll be moving to L.A. shortly."

"Hm. Yeah. I suppose." She took his card and gave him another brilliant smile. Her friend had turned around and frowned at her. She shrugged.

"Thanks," he said.

"Have a great flight."

He got back in line again. She waved. He wasn't sure if the wave was for him or for her friend. Most likely her friend.

When she called him not one but two weeks later, he had all but forgotten their brief encounter, though he recognized her delightful voice and accent right away. At the same time, he was also irritated with all the details of his impending move. This was also the night of his performance in a benefit concert at the Kennedy Center which doubled as a farewell concert for him from the Washington, D.C. music scene. He explained to her how strapped for time he was, but he would happily serve her a cup of coffee. It being his last night in town, he was staying at the Watergate hotel. Could she meet him there? When she agreed, he briefly thought of getting her a complimentary ticket to the night's performance, but he only had her first name, Lara. Would that do? Probably. But because he had so much still to do, he didn't feel like wasting time making phone calls. The important thing was to prepare for his own performance, and once again he felt his focus derailed by this tiny blonde with blue eyes called Lara. He liked the sound of her name.

When reception called up to announce her, he said to send her up. He answered her knock on his door with an impatient "Come in," only to find he had forgotten to unlock the door. So, he had to go to the door, and he spilled a whole sheaf of sheet music in the process.

"Well, here you are," he said, bending down to pick up a few sheets of music from the floor as he ushered her into his suite.

"This is not a good time for me to be here. I can tell." She handed him a bunch of daffodils.

"It's just that I'm leaving tomorrow. Plus, I have a

concert tonight."

"I've looked you up on the internet. Sounds like you're doing well for yourself."

"Yes. So...."

They had moved into his suite but were still standing and seemed at an impasse.

"Play a song for me," she said, "and I'll let you get back to what all you need to do."

"If I do that, will you go to bed with me?"

"No. But thanks for asking." She looked directly into his eyes for a moment and then turned to leave.

"Wait," he called after her, still holding the daffodils in one hand and three sheets of music in the other. "It's just...."

She was gone. He felt fury well up inside him. There hadn't been enough time for finesse. Not two weeks ago. Not now. He felt both reprimanded and ripped off. For once, his favorite meditation technique failed him, though he tried it three times over the next few hours. Anger kept roiling inside him. He couldn't eat, not even his usual pre-performance grapes. The anger was still there when he stepped onto the stage. It was still there when he stepped down from the stage after a standing ovation, which didn't seem particularly exceptional.

"Brilliant....you were on fire....never played like that....that tango sequence....exquisite...." He took in snatches of congratulatory phrases. In one ear, out the other, while he stood in his tuxedo doing the customary hour of hobnobbing, the part of his job that he liked the least. One day he might be famous enough to be able to dispense with that, but he wasn't there yet.

In the morning he read only the review in the Post, skipping the others. It confirmed that he had apparently outdone himself. He thought of calling Lara to thank her. After all, her phone number would be on his phone from when she had called him yesterday. He decided against. Thank her for what exactly? Instead, he deleted her phone number from his call history—he'd always hated the telephone anyway—hoping she would not decide to call him again from her end. After yesterday's debacle, he was reasonably sure she would not.

On the way out the door to meet his limousine to the airport, he noticed he had failed to put the daffodils in water. They lay limp and defeated on the coffee table as he was off into this brilliant future.

Echoes of a Summer

They hadn't seen each other since that summer twenty-eight years ago. Marian was now music director and youth group leader in her church. Ann, a public defender, had never visited the out-of-the-way southwestern town Silver City before and decided to look up her old friend. Sitting outside at the beautifully landscaped Tranquilbuzz Coffee House, with a gentle Zen waterfall gurgling near them, complete with koi in the pool below, they soon reminisced about their magical summer retreat in Pennsylvania all those years ago. Three weeks of lakeside mystery and magic, studying, removing daddy-long-legs from their dormitory walls, and above all their guide, the unforgettable Devin Cooper.

While Marian went inside the coffee house to stand in line for a second round of cappuccinos, Ann recalled her first memory of him. "Call me DC." She couldn't remember why he and she stood at a blackboard where she had drawn a huge white chalk flower with vines coiled all around it. It might have been an assignment. She'd worn a pink wool dress inherited from an older cousin. Why had there only been the two of them? He had looked at her drawing and told her how pretty it was and how he hoped one day all those looped vines would fall away and the flower in the center would be free.

"I was just thinking about first meeting DC," Ann told Marian who placed the two cappuccinos on the wooden bench seat between them. The small table in front of them seemed too long a reach for convenience. "He was my hero," she added. "Still is to this date. I'm sure he made it to heaven. He was much too young. I've always been half in love with him, you know. I'm sure we all were. Most of us anyway." It was a statement as much as a prompt for Marian to chime in with memories of her own. When Marian remained silent, Ann continued, "He had such a knack for always making everyone feel as though they mattered. Well, he made *me* feel important at any rate. Always lifted me up. Not many people have made the effort to do that for me. And, do you remember, when we sat in a circle that summer? You couldn't detect any individual movement, but once he started talking, ten minutes later everybody sat a few inches closer to him."

"You dated his son for a while, didn't you?" Marian asked.

"Yeah. Joey was lovely, too. Joseph." Ann's voice trailed off. She tasted memory in her mouth. "But nothing like his dad." She thought of DC's intense blue eyes, compelling in an unaggressive way. She wished she could look into those eyes just one more time.

"He came on to me, you know," Marian said.

"Joey?" Ann felt heat in her cheeks.

"No. DC."

"What do you mean?" Ann knew what Marian meant. She immediately regretted asking.

"I mean he asked me to go to bed with him," Marian said.

"And did you?" Ann felt her lips stick together. It was difficult to get them apart to speak. It couldn't be true.

"Heck no," Marian said. "Come on. He was what, 30 years older? Something like that? And married."

Questions tumbled helter-skelter through Ann's mind. What did he say to her, or do to her, to make her feel he was coming on to her? Ann couldn't see him as a culprit. The minister at DC's funeral three years ago said he was the most perfect human being he had ever met. No, Marian had to be mistaken. Maybe she was a legend in her own mind, assuming any small friendliness was a come on. And if it was true, then why Marian and not Ann? Who would want to go to bed with Marian anyway? And not Ann? Marian wasn't ugly, but Ann was prettier. She felt abandoned, devastated. Was it fate? Perhaps even benevolently so? Ann had the queasy feeling, had he come on to her, she would have been his for the asking. Never mind age. Never mind marital status. She felt like an outcast. Skipped over. And how could Marian make this all sound so casual? Ann simply didn't want to believe any of it. To have been a fool for not knowing what might have been going on, and on top of that to not be the chosen one.

DC and Ann had exchanged letters for years, even after her short interlude with Joey was over. DC had designed his own stationery, doves and the words for peace in several languages watermarked across the paper. Once, out of the blue, he had sent her a check for Christmas, and she had bought a silver shirt with it which she had worn until it fell apart beyond repair. She didn't now want to be stuck with this secret she had no wish of knowing. Marian must have misunderstood. That had to be it. Twenty-eight years later, and Ann felt achingly dull. A reject. Not chosen. While Marian cavalierly dismissed the memory with her throaty laughter before changing the subject. She must have been wrong.

In the car on the way to a hotel in Tucson, having declined Marian's offer to spend the night, Ann did her best to drive with special care, for this was exactly the sort of situation where she would miss a speed limit change or a stop sign because her mind was swirling elsewhere. She tried to imagine him kissing Marian and could not. She tried to imagine herself kissing him. She couldn't do that either. Still, if it was true at all, why not her? Why not her?

The Answer

Her feet dangled from the low stone wall. Len looked like a young Hemingway, but with the full beard of Hemingway's later years. He hugged his left leg which was drawn up on the wall. His right leg dangled like hers.

A pot of geraniums stood between them, salmon-colored and pungent. The wind kept playing with the scent. "Sally planted those," he said. "You might like them for your balcony. She told me to talk to you. You would know why she left. I need to understand. I love her so much. I thought she loved me too. It's not another man, she says. Then why?"

Once in a while, the wind sent up a spray of mist from the river below. Mary didn't know what to tell him. She felt important and incompetent. Sally was her best friend. Mary had been maid of honor at their wedding less than two years ago. Sally had never complained about Len. Her sudden decision to leave him and move into an efficiency apartment downtown had surprised Mary too, but she hadn't given it much thought. There had been no drama and no apparent pain, at least not on Sally's part. Just a simple decision. Len, meanwhile, seemed to be in great pain. And he was waiting for an answer.

"I don't know, Len," Mary finally said. "I simply don't know. Maybe you were fencing her in. I really don't know."

"But she said to ask you," he insisted.

Mary scrunched her forehead. She thought of her own yearning for freedom, for independence, for making her own way in the world. She wanted to put salve on Len's obvious wound, but she didn't have any.

"I really don't know what to tell you," she finally admitted. "I just don't."

Len let go of his drawn-up leg and looked down into the frothing water. They sat side by side for a long time on either side of the pot of geraniums, not speaking, guarding each other's silence, honoring each other's presence and confusion. She felt closer to him than she had ever felt before. She wanted to protect him.

When night fell, and hunger started asserting itself, and they became aware of the bicycles and dog walkers and yells of children on the path behind them, they finally stood and hugged and went their separate ways.

"I wish I could have helped," she said.

"You did by being here."

Thirty years later he still looked like Hemingway when they met by chance at an airport, both on their hectic way to somewhere else. This prompted Mary to ask Sally when they saw each other again: "What did you mean by telling him to ask me to explain why you left him?"

"I don't remember," Sally said. "I probably just said that. To get him off my back. He was so sad."

Memorable

The last guest left. Finally, as far as Miriam was concerned, though she knew she should be flattered and grateful. It was the first time in her life that friends gave her a surprise farewell party. It was the last time as well, though she wouldn't have known that. Tom and Nick had arranged everything, and the surprise had been genuine. Tom was the local music guru with whom she had somehow developed an occasional lunch friendship, though she had never taken a lesson with him, private or otherwise. Nick was a violinist, poet, and law student who was currently renting a spare bedroom in Tom's penthouse apartment while completing law school. She was staying with them for her last night in the country. Tom had graciously offered his sofa, and the apartment was convenient to the airport by Metro. She only had carry-on luggage. Two footlockers with a few of her most cherished possessions had preceded her to Paris where Bernard, her fiancé of seven years, lived, and where she would join him as of tomorrow. Possibly to get married, though while they had committed to it for some nebulous time in the future, neither of them considered it a very pressing matter. Bernard had promised to help find her flute playing engagements. And she could always give lessons.

She had had a crush on Nick for four years straight, ever since they had been in a chamber music group together. Once early on, Nick had criticized her lack of voicing her opinion in the group, and for some incongruous reason that had spurred her on to try and prove herself to him. It was never quite clear to her whether she had succeeded in that endeavor. At least he was always respectful to her after his first animated critique. Nick, recently divorced, was cheerfully playing the field but, to her puzzlement, never made any overtures to her. His current preoccupation was a frail woman from Philadelphia whom he found fascinating.

Leaving a place, and especially leaving the country,

lent itself to certain liberties, for example to making a proposition without the danger of extreme disgrace to either party, so, after the last guest finally descended down the elevator, she asked him if she could spend the night with him. To her delight, Nick didn't skip a beat and accepted, only mentioning his astonishment at her being so free. He had the back bedroom with just a small window to the river view, but the rent was nominal, and he was supposed to be studying most of the time rather than looking out at the river. Besides, now it was night anyway.

She thought it would only be polite to let Tom know that she would not spend the night on the sofa. She knew all this was not quite in keeping with her general reputation, so she was nervous when she went to say goodnight to Tom who was busy lining up glasses and porcelain dishes by the dishwasher in the kitchen, waving off her involuntary offer to help. Her nervousness made her mouth dry, and it felt as though her lips stuck together when she told Tom in a semi-whisper that she was going to spend the night with Nick. For a moment he misunderstood and thought she was telling him she wanted to spend the night with him. She saw a smug gleam light up his eyes, then fade again as she quickly clarified. It made her feel horrible, for him and for herself as well. For her part, she felt like a teenager wearing a miniskirt to attract attention from her peers, only to get the unwelcome attention of an unattractive elder instead. Tom was in his late sixties. She was not even thirty yet. Currently he was courting a woman only ten years his junior; however, rumor had it this woman had recently declined Tom's marriage proposal for the second time.

Things finally straightened out, she went to Nick's bedroom, still preoccupied by the recent shock to her system. "Spend the night with Nick" didn't sound anything remotely like "spend the night with you," even with compromised lips and teeth. At least so she thought.

She was distracted and felt like an alien when she and Nick finally made love. It was not very memorable. They didn't speak. Nick's penis was fleshier and ruddier than she had imagined. Not that she was an expert on penises, having only encountered two others prior to this event. Somehow her anticipation and imagination had raised her expectation to a level beyond what was on offer in reality. When they considered themselves done, she touched his pockmarked face with tenderness and lay awake for a long time, wondering if his earlier reference to her astonishing freedom meant that he now considered her a slut, or whether it meant that, had he had that knowledge earlier, he might have taken a chance on falling in love with her. Overall, the most memorable part of the occasion had been the glint of self-satisfaction in Tom's eyes when he had first misunderstood her intentions.

Paris was wonderful and exceeded expectations with plenty of opportunities for earning her keep with her flute, and she married Bernard in due course.

Nick became a successful lawyer, and his music and poetry faded into the background of the demands of business.

A few years later, Tom married a woman even younger than Miriam.

Yearning Curve

The first time they danced was on the second Wednesday in April. She noted it in her diary. They danced four sets, well, three and a half, as the first set was already under way by the time he asked her to dance. Etiquette suggested that he circulate and dance with other women of which there typically were more than men. He didn't, and she didn't mind at all. His name was Santiago, Santi to friends, and to her his skillful leads felt like coming home. He made it all feel so easy. Suddenly and unexpectedly, she was in love with the weeping violins of the music. Suddenly she felt that the whole mystique of tango was not a mistake, not a trap, and not a cliché. Well maybe a cliché, but one that got to be that way on merit. He smelled of vetiver.

"Do you come here often?" he asked during a break in the music.

"Sometimes," she said.

"I haven't seen you before. Do you go to other places?"

"No, but I'm thinking about it."

"Please," he said with a small nod. He mentioned two other places he liked to go, one on Mondays, one on Fridays. Then the music started again. She no longer noticed who else was there that night or whether there were flowers on the tables, and she never once worried about her mascara running.

For two long days afterwards, her mind was fuzzy and sang strange songs of soft exuberance.

Normally she limited her dancing to once a week. There were so many other things to do. That week, however, she went again on Friday, and they danced again. He danced a few sets with other women between dances with her. She felt secure all the same. It was obvious that, like her, he didn't have a regular dance partner. She started looking forward to a wonderful summer. He told her his favorite song, but, as it wasn't played that night, she forgot by the time she got home. She would ask him to remind her when they danced again. She started planning what to wear next Wednesday, black chiffon pants probably and a shoulder-bearing black sequin top, as she was proud of her shoulders. And a red chiffon scarf to match her sparkling spirit.

Walking by the sea, she had many imaginary conversations with him. Dozens of times she replayed in her mind just how he had led a simple *ocho*, then a *molinete*, then a *volcada*, and how wonderful it felt to respond to his perfect touch, his expert leads.

The next Wednesday he wasn't there. Or the following Friday or Monday. She kept hoping he would come. He didn't.

For weeks she recorded in her diary that dancing was okay, but Santi didn't come. She missed him. Summer came and went. One Friday in July, she danced with someone whose looks reminded her of Santi, but it wasn't the same. She stayed until one set after midnight and looked at the moon out of one of the tall windows of the top floor dance venue.

One day in the kitchen she mentioned to her roommate how Santi had effectively spoiled every other dance partner for her, even the excellent ones.

"So, ask some of the other dancers," her roommate suggested. "Something like, there's this guy named Santi. Do you know where he goes?"

"But I do know where he goes. He told me. And I've gone there. Except he hasn't been."

"Oh, well, one day you will run into him again."

Listening to her roommate's words, she realized that if she passed Santi on the street, she possibly wouldn't even recognize him now. She missed him and his dancing, that was true. But she missed her original enchantment with him even more.

Suddenly, one Wednesday in late September, he was there again. Of course they danced, and they danced well. And it was way too late. The bloom was off. Reality fell flat.

It puzzled her, but not overly much. She'd never been all that good at reality anyway. She thought of asking where he had been but decided against it. He told her again his favorite song, *Amanacer*. This time she would remember. Anyone who claimed it was never too late was wrong. There really was such a thing as too late, one of the saddest concepts in all the world, and she had no choice but to capitulate to its desiccated feeling.

Winter slid around the corner, and it was long. No more rhapsody, just the mutual politeness of disappointment and compassion. Dance felt like an elaborate game in which people avoided the truth with elegant maneuvers, trying to keep the appearance of magic alive. One Monday night, she watched and listened to an old man playing the bandoneon. Haunting melodies that ached with sadness and beauty. One other night someone kissed her hand. She couldn't afterwards remember if it was Santi or not. She missed her yearning and was filled with shadow. She wanted to be grateful and instead she felt the cool claw of indifference.

On the second Wednesday in April the following year, she said goodbye to Santi. She was moving out of town. She wanted to bring him a rose and then thought better of it. For one thing, she wasn't even sure he'd be there. But he was, and they danced, and that was that. All done. It wasn't as though she hadn't been warned. Tango was a melancholy sort of thing, made of desire and glitter and sinuous and fragrant dreams that faded with reality into an acquired taste of *if only*.

At the Foot of the Mountain

Daniel was still surprised, pleased too, each time there was no cloud of cigarette smoke to greet him when he opened the door to the lounge. Just the scent of piñon incense remained. In the past, it had been used to cover up the smoke, now it was pure ornament. The big fireplace rustled with artificial logs. He felt good. He usually did. He was one of the lucky ones who was confident that people always liked him. He looked around. Two tables were occupied, one by a vivacious woman in pink and gray and a child, the second by a hooded person with a pair of crutches leaning against a chair. There were two more tables closer to the fireplace, empty, but he chose a stool at the bar. So far, none of the other stools were taken.

He'd come here for seven years and couldn't remember now when the place had changed over from smoking to non-smoking. Maybe three or four years ago. Rita was still with him then. They had first met in this lounge seven years ago, right here at the bar. He'd been sitting over his mulled wine, which was called glow wine or glue wine, something like that. His mental association had been something sticky, although the drink itself was smooth velvet.

He started watching the room through the mirror over the bar. The woman in pink and gray used large gestures and was dressed theatrically. Elegant, though. Gorgeous face. Huge eyes. Gray sweater. Pink pashmina wrapped around her neck with both ends falling forward over perky breasts. Her lipstick matched the shawl. Diamond studs in her ears. The little girl beside her in a pink anorak was less attractive, a bit pudgy, but she wore purple earmuffs with sequins. You had to hand her that.

The hoodie person sat hunched forward, face hidden entirely. Slight build—with the gloomy disposition of a surly teenager. A touch comical, too. Clearly a person who wanted to be left alone with his or her mulled wine or beer or cider or whatever it was.

Rita, seven years ago, had swept into this lounge, carrying cool breeze in with her, and sat down on the barstool beside him.

"It's the only seat left," she'd said. "D'you mind? I'm Rita."

"Daniel." He'd lifted himself two inches off his stool. "Denial to my friends." Stupid thing to say, but he couldn't just then think of anything else.

Her laughter had been precious. "I prefer Daniel."

Daniel now reached for a handful of salted peanuts from one of several bowls sitting on the counter.

The pink and gray woman's child looked bored and brooding and plotting. Mom, or whatever their relationship was, looked disdainful. Not sisters, he thought.

The hoodie person never seemed to move at all, though over time the level of drink before him or her seemed to diminish. Female. Something said female, but not very strongly so. Maybe the lean body.

"Glow wine," Daniel ordered when the bartender finally gave him her attention. She looked underage but obviously had to be legal to be working there.

"Beg your pardon?" she asked.

"Umh—do you have mulled wine? You used to." In fact, he thought he could smell it.

"Mulled wine coming right up," she said. She disappeared through a door to the left of the bar and returned with a steaming glass mug reinforced by a metal band below its handle. "Yeah, I remember now. They told me they used to call it something else. Management changed, you know."

"Staff too, I believe?" he said.

"Yes, I'm new this season."

She was nice to look at. Brown doe eyes. But he didn't want to chat. Besides, she was too young. And he had come to remember, to think, to make sense of life. He felt as though, if he were to turn around, Rita would step into the lounge, so much did he feel her presence. But Rita was gone.

Earlier that afternoon he had walked on their mountain—not as far up as he had hiked with her in years past. Alone he didn't want to venture too far up without backup. Not that backup was necessarily useful as he knew only too well.

He sipped his mulled wine. He preferred calling it glow wine. It's what it felt like, gentle warm glow filling his mouth, going down with a bit of spice, making him dreamy.

It had been Rita's favorite winter drink too.

Today on the mountain there hadn't been any snow on the ground except a scattering of old dark rimmed deposits of refrozen snow in the shadows of overhangs on the path.

Last year there had been another blizzard and he had gone only a few hundred yards before turning around.

"Are you all right over there?" the bartender asked.

"Fine, fine," he said. "But I wouldn't mind if you brought me another later."

He knew he shouldn't guzzle it too fast. Dreamy was okay. Even maudlin was okay to a point. But he didn't want to become drowsy. Not in public. He could of course charm the bartender into giving him a supply of the wine to take to his room, but the point was to be in public. Here. To let go. To process. Whatever it took.

In the mirror he saw the pink and gray woman and her daughter had been joined by a stuffy looking guy in an ill-fitting dark suit. A light buzz hung in the air, low voices and crackling fire. A friendly hum. The hoodie person was still there too—hands wrapped around a glass like his own.

His life would be okay now. He felt free. He had never exactly felt unfree, but heavy from the events of the past. The blizzard. The loss.

Perfume reminiscent of agreeable incense preceded the woman who slid onto the barstool on his left. He looked at her sideways as she brushed something from her knee-high brown leather boots. Long blond hair fell copiously as she bent to her side. When she straightened up, he couldn't look away fast enough to pretend he hadn't been checking her out.

"Hi," she said. "My name is Mandy." Stunning brown eyes, larger even than Rita's whose eyes he had once referred to as large windows of a large soul.

"I'm Daniel," he said.

She waved over the bartender to order a hot buttered rum, then turned to Daniel again. "Are you here alone?"

Wait, Daniel thought, that's supposed to be my line. Her confident directness made him smile. "I am," he said. "You?"

Her hot buttered rum arrived in a glass mug like Daniel's.

"You're here for the non-existing skiing?" She raised her eyebrows. She hadn't answered his question.

"I come every year at this time," he said. "An anniversary of sorts."

"A solo anniversary?"

He didn't reply.

"Sorry," she said. "That was probably rude."

"'S okay."

"Anyway, I'm here to savor breaking up with an inadequate boyfriend. Pre-season the lodgings were cheap, and I needed to get away."

She looked attractive. Striking really. But he had reservations. She felt a bit forward. Effusive. The child with the woman in pink and gray started to stand up, but the woman stopped her by holding on to her arm. The girl sat back down and started singing "ring around the rosie" in an annoyingly loud voice. He wished the woman would have let her go wherever she had wanted to go.

"Sorry to hear that," he said to Mandy. "About the boyfriend and the inadequacy. Not the cheap lodgings and the getaway."

"Yeah. Well. One of those things." She opened her brown eyes wide which made them look like sunflower centers. "The path of life, you know. So, tell me about this anniversary of yours. Obviously if you're here alone, it doesn't have anything to do with a woman. Or a man." She gave him a speculative glance. He took it as a compliment. To get the benefit of doubt as to possibly being gay on purely physical evidence had to be flattering.

"It does actually. My love—I don't know what else to call her. We weren't married, so she wasn't my wife. We met here. And then—I lost her. Here. Two years ago."

He saw curiosity in her face, like a camera shutter opening to capture a view. Suddenly she looked delectable to him, all wide-eyed and serious and encouraging. Her left knee was crossed over her right knee now, pointing toward him. He noticed a small commotion behind them. The pink and gray woman was leaving, together with pudgy child and stuffy man. Now, that one would have been more his type. But here was this glorious blonde beside him, with brown sunflower eyes. He wondered if her hair color was real.

"So, tell me your story," Mandy said. They'd been sitting side by side in silence for a few moments.

In the mirror, he still watched the woman in pink and gray. She was the last of the three out through the door.

"I haven't looked at a woman ever since." He laughed. "Well, you know what I mean." He looked at Mandy as though he might just make an exception for her. It was a combination of wine—his glass was almost empty, and he waved to the bartender to replenish it—and her warm eyes.

"It was our fifth year here," he began." We came every year on this date—ever since we first met here." He spoke to her sympathetic eyes now, and to the glow in his own chest from the warmth of the jewel-toned wine.

"I left her in the snow. A blizzard. She disappeared. I left her there. In the blizzard. We weren't prepared. I wanted to avoid the worst of it, so I stepped out as we rushed down the mountain. No, we didn't have skis or snowshoes or anything. We were just out for a hike, and we were caught in a surprise storm. We had even watched the weather report earlier, and it was sunny when we set out. We saw beautiful vistas. We were way up, you see. Then the unexpected clouds rolled in at unbelievable speed from the east."

"More mulled wine?" the bartender asked. "Sorry it took so long to get back to you."

"Yes. Thanks," he said, then, "You really want to hear this, Mandy?"

"I do." Her eyes looked friendly. She put a hand on his arm. "What happened?"

"She must have twisted her ankle. Or broken it. That's all. I felt so guilty. Still do. She'd called several times for me to wait up, to slow down. My legs being longer than hers. And I was heavier, so I had more traction. I'd slow down briefly, then pick up my pace again. By now the snow was coming down practically sideways. The wind was biting. I wanted to be out of there. Suddenly I heard her cry out behind me. Again. I was impatient. Angry almost. That she couldn't keep up. I turned around. 'Come on,' I called to her. 'We've got to get out of here.' She was sitting on the ground. This was no time for theatrics, I thought. Damn her. 'Come on,' I yelled. She didn't get up. Dark blob in the white snow. The snow still came down sideways. 'Can't,' she yelled back. Or something like that. So, I hiked back to her. Fifty yards, maybe more. I hated to. It was so cold. I mean, we were dressed adequately. At least we were that prepared. But it was still darn cold. I wanted to coax her to get on with it. I thought she had just lost heart, from exhaustion. But it was worse. She couldn't stand. I tried to handle her leg to figure out what to do. I'm no medical genius, though. I didn't know what I was doing. She just screamed through her ski mask when I touched her leg, so I stopped. Meanwhile the snow kept coming. Our eyelashes were frozen. 'I guess we're not going to make it down the mountain,' I said. Meaning we were going to die up here. Freeze to death. I wasn't going to be able to carry her. Not all the way. Not in that blizzard. And I didn't know how we would make it through the night if I stayed with her. And in the morning? Then what? God, I didn't want to die. I felt so alive, so full of future.

"She gave me this long sad look. Maybe not all that long. In the snow it felt like it lasted forever. And it did in a way, 'cause I have never forgotten that look. Sad, haunted.

And loving, too. 'You go on,' she said. 'You can make it. I can't.' 'Maybe I can get help,' I said. 'Yes,' she said. We both knew it was not likely. It could take me hours to get down to the lodge. It was getting darker now, too, from night closing in, not just from the storm. 'I should stay with you,' I said. Just recently we had made each other a promise of sorts how, if one of us got in trouble, we would stay together.

"There was this very tired look in her eyes. Not betrayal, not anger, just extreme sadness and weariness. A hollow look. 'Go on, you,' she said. 'There's no point in both of us staying and freezing.' I should have stayed. I know that. I knew it fifty steps away, a hundred steps away. I so wanted to live, and she had told me to go. Still, I should have stayed. I think she would have stayed with me. I can't even imagine how lonely she must have felt when I left. I didn't turn back. My heart was yearning for life. I did pray for her all the way down."

Daniel's eyes sought Mandy's for reassurance. How lovely it would have been to hear, *You did the right thing. You could neither live for her, nor die for her.* Mandy's eyes were squinted slits. Considering, judging, and perhaps not judging kindly. He felt betrayed. He shouldn't ever have trusted anyone with his truth, much less a total stranger. There was no mercy in this world.

"When I got back the next morning with a rescue crew just short of dawn," he said, "there was no sign of her. She had simply disappeared. She was clean gone. Not a shred of clothing. No blood. Nothing. We dug in the area in the snow. We should have found her, or some sign of her. But there was nothing. Just miles and miles of deep fresh snow. I did what I could, and she was gone. It's been two years. There will always be a shrine to her in my heart. You see, in a way, my life, my being here now, is a gift from her."

The sympathetic look he still hoped for from Mandy didn't materialize. He had lost her somehow. Her eyes were shifty now. A cold fume started building inside him. Why should he be condemned when all he wanted was to live?

He forced himself to smile. "I shocked you. I

disappointed you," he said.

Mandy looked at him directly now. "It's not that," she said, then shifted her glance away again. "There's a woman at the table behind us. She's making me uneasy. She's staring at us. She's been staring at us all this time."

Daniel looked into the mirror over the bar. The woman's hoodie had come off as he was talking. Her face looked blotched, unsmiling. Her eyes were luminous.

"I made it down," she said.

The Photograph

Talking to my husband on the cell phone after boarding the plane put me on edge. That's how it always is. It's not my fault either. Dave is so slow, and so incompetent.

And no matter what he says, I know for a fact that I'm a very pleasant person. I've always been pleasant and always will be. Always. Everyone I ask says I'm easy to get along with. But he so irritates me.

So, it was no wonder that everything else annoyed me a bit as well. My seat neighbor first of all. She dragged her skinny butt in late enough to claim her window seat so that we all had to stand up again and let her squeeze in, with her purse slapping my knee as she pulled herself into the row.

Next, she intrigued me. She was constantly writing.

Now of course I wish I hadn't been quite so intrigued because eventually she turned to the back of her notebook. Did I mention she wrote long-hand? She had a laptop, too, but she only turned it on once and then turned it right off again.

This woman was nothing special to look at, mind you. I guess I mostly noticed her because she was constantly fidgeting, tray table down to write on it for a while, tray table up to write on her lap, turning her knees this way, then that way, constantly doing something or other. Although I must admit, she never did intrude on my space. Not physically anyway.

I had once dreamt of being a writer myself. But that was when I was much younger.

She was older than I, of course. By about ten years, I'd say. About Dave's age in fact. I distinctly remember thinking this, even before anything else happened, that she was about his age. An ordinary middle-aged woman. And, also like Dave, Caucasian. White. The winner race.

So I thought—daydreaming, as one does when flying

and there isn't anything else to do in that cramped space—maybe she's a famous writer. Maybe I'm sitting here right next to a famous writer.

That was ridiculous of course. If she were a famous writer, why, then she'd hardly be sitting back here with the likes of me in Economy. That didn't occur to me then, though. What occurred to me was that pleasant little fantasy of her sitting there, right next to me, possibly being famous.

A couple of times I thought of asking her what she was writing. In fact, I spent a good twenty minutes weighing the pros and cons of that. Finally, of course, the urge always went away again. I mean, you don't just simply ask people questions like that, especially not when they are obviously busy, and on top of everything potentially famous.

The latest wave of "I'll ask her after all" was just about to crest when she flipped to the back of her notebook. There was some writing on the last page, just a few lines, and she started adding to that, scribbling in the same fast and furious manner as before.

Then I noticed there was a photograph glued into the back cover of the notebook, on the inside, facing that last page.

Sweet, I thought. Like having a photo of your husband and children on the desk in your office, or something like that. Obviously someone she loved.

That's when I saw it was a photograph of my husband.

No, I didn't want to believe it either. So I kept looking. Again. And again. It was him—unless he has an identical twin whom nobody had ever heard of somewhere in the world—and one who wears the same clothes. Because I sure recognized the shirt. It's been in the laundry often enough. We share laundry duties. One week he does it. The next week I have to.

When I was sure it was him, I felt like somebody held a hot iron to my chest. I mean, what was I to do? Cause a scene in mid-flight? In this day and age of terrorist scares?

But in my imagination, I grew to twice my size and

towered over her. "Why, you bitch, you."

Whatever cuss words I could think of weren't bad enough. My skin prickled with a fever to do something. But in reality, I just broke into a sweat and sat there, doing nothing. That's right. Nothing.

Except pretty soon I started looking at her again, studying her. She really was ordinary, just as I had thought before. Nothing special. Mid-fortyish, plain-looking, Caucasian, no gray in her hair. If it was a dye job, it was a damn good one, 'cause there were no roots, and the color looked real.

Suddenly she smiled, all dreamy, and she looked up from the page. No, not at me. She turned to the window and smiled into the windowpane. For quite a while.

She seemed completely absorbed, so I craned a bit to see if I could make out any of the writing in the notebook in her lap, but I couldn't.

That bastard, I thought. Because, you see, Dave is not famous or anything. Quite the opposite. And here was this woman flying around with a notebook with his picture glued in the inside back cover.

There were only two ways she could have a photo of him. He had either given it to her, or she had taken it herself, and either way meant that she knew him. Which of course wouldn't be the whole story either, because, well, obviously, I know a lot of people myself, and I don't necessarily tote around pictures of them, do I now?

I looked at her hands. No ring.

She still stared at the window, and her face went through a series of expressions. Nice expressions, happy expressions. Unbelievable.

Was she thinking of Dave? Or one of her other lovers, the little slut? Though there was only his picture in the back of her notebook, mind you.

I started making speeches in my head, addressed to no one in particular. Some kind of jury. I want you to know, he's a total loser. Yes, a complete loser. I'm only sorry that he came into my life in the first place. I have no respect for him. He's gentle, maybe, and that's about that on the positive side. Makes no money to speak of. Yeah, right, famous! When I say quite the opposite, that's how it is, and then some. He can't provide. He doesn't do anything right. Probably thinks he's being wonderful by sharing laundry duties. Like hell. He doesn't even know how to put the detergent in—after the water has started filling, and not before. I mean, you could ruin a whole load that way.

And I had to personally train him to leave the toilet seat down. I mean, didn't he have a mother? Was he sick when they taught manners? And he has hairs in his nose that he doesn't always clip. And, can you believe it, he marks up perfect books with highlights and underlining. Nobody ever taught him about taking notes, or what? Or making copies and putting your marks on those?

He's a newspaper photographer. And, boy, oh boy—not that he makes a great deal of money with it. But his precious equipment, boy, oh boy. If you so much as breathe on it, all hell breaks loose.

"I'd like you to handle these with care," he'll say, with that benevolent and patronizing and infuriating twinkle in his eyes, "Or tell me if it's in your way, and I'll move it myself."

As though he's ever around when his damn stuff is in the way.

Meanwhile, if it comes to making food, I mean, preparing it, I finally got him to wrap up lunch sandwiches properly. And he does know how to make a decent cup of tea. Though I had to throw out a few of them when he didn't catch the water just when it got to a boil. That's right, straight down the sink in front of his eyes. He had to learn sooner or later.

How anybody could tolerate him, or care for him, or even love him is beyond me. I should know. I tried.

But he's mine, and no smiling idiot sitting in an airplane next to me has a right to have his photo in her notebook. I'd rather kill him. Than what? I don't know. I wish I had the nerve to throw some coffee on her lap, on her notebook, on his photograph.

What will I do when I get home, Dave? You'll suffer
for this. Somebody has to. Because now you will love
someone else the way you have never loved me, and I don't
want you, it's far too late for that, but I don't want someone
else to have what I once wanted from you either. All I wanted
was love. This is defeat. And I cannot bear it. My tears are
choking me.

Something Important

"Daddy, are you going to ask her to...?"

"Tssssss...." Tammy put her hand over her twin sister Sammy's mouth, her arm snaked all the way around her sister's shoulders in the back seat of the car. They'd only recently graduated from booster seats to seat belts. "We're not supposed to pry."

"I'm not prying," Sammy mumbled against her sister's hand without biting. "I just want to know."

"Look, three bald eagles up on the right," Mary called out from the front passenger seat to distract the twins. David, driving, had told her before they got into the car that he had something important to tell her later on, and the girls, who probably were not expected to pay attention to the adults, had heard it. Now, though, both girls leaned right to look out of the window.

"I see them."

"Me too."

"Daddy, don't look. Keep your eyes on the road."

That seemed to have been the end of the issue for them. Not for Mary, however. What was she going to do if he did ask? Forty-seven percent of her was yes. Fifty-three percent was no. Much like their divided country. She wanted to keep things as they were for a long time to come. It was comfortable. Part of her, however, also wanted guarantees, and their current situation held no guarantees. Everything seemed a bit divided these days. Except for the twins who seemed to move through the world like a well-oiled unit. Perhaps in small ways, though, they too were divided. Sammy usually hurled herself into the world with boisterous energy. Tammy more often put on the brakes of prudent obedience.

They reached the twin's mother's building. Everybody looked up to see if she was standing on the balcony waiting for them or even waving. She was not. She rarely was. Mary couldn't think of a single time, though of course she wasn't always part of the transfer. David stopped on the curb. The girls spilled out of their respective car doors, unicorn backpacks in hand, with shoulder straps trailing on the ground. Sammy's backpack was red, Tammy's blue, and the unicorns faced opposite directions, Sammy's right, Tammy's left. Other than that, they glittered identically with rhinestones Mary had recently glued into their manes and on the tips of their horns.

"Did you check the seat to make sure you have everything?" David asked. He was out of the car as well. Mary stayed in her seat, just in case they were observed from above after all. She didn't want to cause undue consternation.

"Got everything."

"Yes, Dad."

"Well then, give us a hug," he said.

"Give *me* a hug," Sammy corrected. "You're the singular. We're the plural."

"Okay, then give *me* a hug, Sammy-Tammy."

They sandwiched him between them, backpacks now on their shoulders.

"Daddy, we love you mo...."

"Tssssss.... We're not supposed to say that."

"Supposed, shmosed."

"But it's...."

"Okay. Fine. But you know anyway, Daddy."

"Bye, Mary!"

"See you next Friday!"

Mary waved from the passenger seat, and off they went into the hallway of their mother's building, holding hands while the unicorns faced each other on their backs.

"What a pair," David said when he pulled back into traffic. Mary kept her eyes fixed out the window, trying not to anticipate, trying to be as indifferent as possible. He, however, seemed to have forgotten that he was going to tell her something important. Or else he was taking his time to gather his own wits.

When they got home, his ex-wife called with a

complaint that they hadn't washed the twins' hair.

Much later that evening, David and Mary sat together by the fireplace, he in the rocking chair reading *The Smithsonian*, she on the carpet reading a novel. At some point he came to sit beside her. She kept on reading. Pretending to in any case. All her nerve endings were busy coping with his presence. He placed his hand on hers. The skin on her arm, all the way up to her elbow, became vivid sensation. Sensations always seemed to concentrate right there, hairs practically standing up.

"There's something important I want to say to you. Have wanted to all afternoon. I'm glad you played Parcheesi with us again today. Thank you for that. I thought after yesterday's fiasco with me being competitive and practically accusing the girls of cheating, you'd never play with us again. I know you were upset. They knew, too. I think it was great for them to see that detestable behavior in an adult, in anyone really, can be forgiven. You're an excellent role model. But most of all it was important for me to see that you can accept me for who I am."

"Oh, that," she said and pulled her hand away from under his. "And now I want to finish reading my novel."

The Wedding

He found her on the terrace behind a row of fragrant lilacs, mascara staining her cheeks.

"The piglets," he said.

"Yes," she said. She pressed her cheek into his white shirt, mascara and all. "Even salamanders in love would have been better. Don't know if I should laugh or cry."

"Both. And talk to me. If you want."

"I didn't even want to have her there. But you can't very well not invite your own mother to your wedding."

"It's been known to happen."

"When I asked her to read a poem at our wedding, I wanted to honor her. What I had in mind was something like Shakespeare or Barrett Browning, not some doggerel about piglets in love. We deserve Shakespeare. And then those rose quartz piglets."

"Such a valuable wedding present," he said, then, imitating her mother's voice, he raised his to a high breathy story-telling pitch. "*They're considered lucky in many cultures. I want you two to have all the luck in the world.*" Then in his normal voice: "With her in the mix, we need it."

Giggles interrupted her sobs. Her cheek was still pressed into his white shirt. "Dad had this mildly disdainful half-smile on his face as though to signal to the world: *See? This is why I'm no longer with her.*"

"He must have experienced his fair share of her benevolent sabotage. Or unfair share, as the case may be."

"That's it. That's exactly it. Benevolent sabotage. With the flowers, too, earlier today. Kelly agreed to do the flower arrangements at cost. Because she's my friend. They were supposed to be Mom's treat, so I let her do the organizing. I was there when Mom talked to her on the phone and said something about white roses and white lilies. I heard it myself, and I was surprised. Mom never liked lilies. Then when the flowers arrived this morning, Mom was all indignant. 'I told her I hate lilies.' Must have been her mysterious whisper voice. Cause I heard 'white lilies' too, not 'hate lilies.' So, Kelly said there'd be no charge for the flowers."

"I know. And it's taken care of. I paid Kelly for the flowers. She argued at first but then did accept in the end."

"Oh, wow." She looked up from his chest into his eyes. "Oh, thank you. I already felt terrible for having wedding flowers with bad karma. And I don't mind white lilies in the least. She doesn't mean to hurt anyone, you know. Mom, that is."

He raised his eyebrows.

"No, really. She's just clumsy, despite all her obvious sophistication. I always feel like a country bumpkin next to her elegance."

"A piglet rather than a princess?"

"Something like that."

"You look nothing like a piglet to me. Shall I compare thee…?"

Her mascara-stained face was about to disappear into his shirt again when she noticed the smudges. "Now I've ruined your shirt on top of everything."

"If we have to explain it, which we don't, we'll chalk it up to wedding emotions. Maybe we shouldn't even go back in. Leave surreptitiously. I'm sure it's the sophisticated custom somewhere in the world for honeymooners to just take off. Let all the guests get drunk and silly on their own. And it appears we have every right to *piggy*back on such traditions."

She laughed out loud, then slowly turned her head from side to side and interlaced her right hand with his left. "What I am really afraid of is that one fine day she'll come after you with her—what did you call it? Benevolent sabotage? And it can really hurt. I don't ever want you hurt."

"I didn't marry her. I married you."

She let go of his hand and picked up the flowing lace of her dress with both hands to make walking easier.

"Let's go cut some cake and then split."

Honeymoon

He said, "come live with me on the mainland," and she started packing. No furniture of course, and she downsized with respect to other things as well. Mere things were so unimportant compared to him. She thought of Rumi and his recommendation to give it all for a kiss.

From time to time, she still feels a favorite CD she left behind vibrate in her memory, and that yellow dance dress with black rhinestones. All for a man? Yes, of course. He is worth it.

She doesn't like to insist on her stuff with him around. She wanted to buy a bread pan yesterday to bake, of all things, stuffed trout. He didn't think it would work. It would. She had done it in the past. It was delicious. Maybe it will all change once she has a job and doesn't have to worry about her savings dwindling to nothing.

She has heard so many versions of "no, no, no" in less than a week. She misses her solitary dreams of him. Pots and pans have to be stainless steel. Most things have to be done twice. At least. Or so it seems.

She can't burn the scented candle she bought. She can't burn incense. He doesn't like it, though he once burned incense on her balcony when he visited her in her island apartment. But that was outside, he explained. She feels strangled by vines of rules. She feels she is getting smaller. She doesn't think she is going to be as happy as she had dreamed.

She wants to cook rice, but he has lent his rice cooker to someone, and it isn't back yet. He doesn't think she should just cook it on the stove top, not when he owns this handy rice cooker. She wants to do laundry, but it is not a convenient time. She prefers liquid detergent. He prefers powder.

He tells her of a woman who showed him how to sensually wash feet on the occasion of inviting him to sleep with her. That young lady was working at a cafeteria when he returned his tray and asked him to wait for her. Her shift was going to be over in fifteen minutes. His new wife doesn't quite understand why he tells her this story or why he tells it to her now.

She asks if they could do things his way one week, then hers the next. He doesn't say yes or no. He doesn't want to commit to that, would rather keep things fuzzy.

She feels she is not civilized enough for him. She wants to run away. She knows she will not, at least not immediately.

She knows she will always love him. Even though everything is complicated and subject to endless negotiation. She doesn't want to negotiate. She only wants to love and to please. She knows things about the world he will never know.

She trembles when he closes the door to his room, afraid she has done something wrong, and she doesn't know what it is. She fears she must get tough. She doesn't want to get tough. She misses the scent of her candles. He used to bring candles when he came to visit her. They were not scented, that's true. He apologizes for the restrictions he places on her.

She doesn't like jazz music, but he loves it.

He ties his shoelaces on the bumper of the car, but when she does it, he tells her to be careful not to scratch anything.

Her life lifts up and drifts away from her. Her laughter drifts away into the world. They are still squabbling over aluminum versus stainless steel and her fears of pleasing or not pleasing. He pre-heats cups before filling them with coffee. Where does he come up with all the time for that sort of thing?

She came with the illusion that he loved her. Now she isn't sure if she will ever be good enough company for him or any other human being. She came with such hopes, and now her candle scent is too strong.

They talk. They talk again. They do not stop talking.

Will it always be her lot to bend? Fortunately, she is very flexible.

She looks forward to when he has to go back to the office and she gets to go back out into the world to look for a job.

The Anniversary

Dear Kevin,

You walked by the rose on the table. I watched you. I saw you pause. "Did I give that to her?" You might have praised it then, its strong red swirl in the center, contained in vivid blue glass. I watched you decide that, no, you hadn't given it to me.

You were correct.

It was a dazzling day with unexpected sun. I walked before dark. I met squirrels and dogs. I hoped for an eagle and celebrated shining crows instead.

I haven't seen anyone in love for a very long time. I used to notice these youngsters all the time, sliding arms around each other, heads moving in the direction of a kiss. Is it me, or is it just winter?

Today we are married ten years. I thought my world would change. It did.

You remember the names of countless senators and foreign dignitaries and football stars. You remember the names of layers of rock in the Grand Canyon. You remember greetings in at least twelve languages. You remember James Joyce's birthday. For whom do you remember these things? Who will admire you when you recite your hard facts?

Ten years ago, I blazed with promise. I would always love you. I have kept this promise, as I always will. Today I will not speak of it to you, though it feels lonely to recite my knowledge to the brook below the bridge behind the recreation center.

If I told you, you might rush around and jump through hoops. But I don't want you like a tiger doing homework in the circus, leaping through flames, or roaring on demand. Indifference is deadly, yes. Still, I don't want it traded for apologetic drill.

I admire everything about you. Blue eyes. Strong

51

shoulders. Exquisite mind. How you complete the New York Times crossword puzzle without cheating. How your hair gleams in sunlight. Your skin against the marbled motion of the sky. Your voice with a background of water. The way you touch the back of my neck.

Today I am exhausted from the endless effort of hope.

I wonder what threatens you to keep you so aloof, adorned with the rote memory of rock formations. Limestone. Coconino sandstone. And still you are, as always, the Bright Angel on my trail.

Today I will not show you memories or celebrations. You don't care, or not enough, and I can't care for you.

Thank you for starting the fire. I treasure the glow, the coarse solidity of silence.

Love,
Robin

Love in the Afternoon

She was long aware that there was a certain ambiguity in wanting attention. Like this, for example. She was, as often, settled sideways into a corner on the sofa, legs drawn up, in the combination kitchen entertainment nook under the large three-pane window and opposite the TV that nobody watched anymore after the kids had gone off to college, except for the occasional National Geographic program Darren might watch. She could straighten out the bookcase over by the balcony door. After the kids had departed with their assorted Kafka, Hegel, Sartre, Shakespeare, Atwood, Oliver, and Morrison, what remained in the bookcase were his star atlases and books about the geology of the Grand Canyon, or water in the desert, or the behavior of beavers. Oh, and there was still the sex manual he had declared "a bit flowery," at which point she had refused looking at it with him again. A bit flowery just didn't seem to be his thing. She'd go donate it to the library one of these days. Together with his copy of some manual on massive extended orgasm. But no, that one wasn't hers to donate. It belonged to him.

She should probably clean the kitchen instead of reading. They never got around to it during the week except for putting things in the dishwasher which they then ran once or twice. But this afternoon she didn't feel like sorting out anything. It was Saturday after all. The cat snuggled into the blanket between her left thigh and the sofa cushion. She spent some moments stroking the cat's back and looking across at the tall Douglas fir trees beyond the narrow community garden that was maintained by the Homeowner's Association. Everything seemed to be stretching up with anticipation of summer. Lovely to think that something was alive out there that didn't depend on seasons and that only grew taller with age.

They had been living amicably side by side for such a long time now, she and Darren. She longed for him to consider her central in his life. She longed for him to ask her questions about herself. It wasn't that they didn't talk to each other. It was just that their interests were so different. When they had first met, she had imagined they would be breathlessly in each other's pocket all the time, walk in the mountains, lie side by side in meadows tickling each other with blades of grass, or by the ocean, holding hands, listening to the water rake the pebbles in its retreat away from shore. She had imagined the two of them touching and talking and totally riveted by what the other one did. Or thought. Or read. Once, in the early days, she had asked him for a list of his favorite books. She had read four of them right away. They didn't exactly float her boat, much less so than Kafka and Sartre or James Joyce, all of whom she had once devoured with fascination when she still had the energy and curiosity of youth and the need to prove her intellectual worth to the world. Once she tried reading her favorite respectable book of all out loud to him, Doris Lessing's *The Marriages Between Zones Three, Four, and Five.* He looked patient and benevolent but not keenly captivated, so she gave that up after two evenings. Since he never returned the favor of asking for a list of her favorite books, she felt she was off the hook as far as his interests were concerned. In return she left him off the hook as well. He just wasn't all that interested in her, or in what she read, or what she felt, and that's the way it was. The end.

These days she didn't even bother to put her journals out of sight. Her private thoughts, which she recorded almost daily, were unquestionably safe from him, although she found that hard to understand. And then again, maybe not. Once she had visited a girlfriend's cabin for a solo retreat and came across a personal journal which she read, including some thoughts on longing for intimacy in lieu of bread and butter sex. It was all a bit boring. Nothing like Anaïs Nin. Then again neither were her own journals anything to crow about. A helter-skelter of yearnings, daily irritations, a recent shopping list for a special anniversary dinner which she might or might not put together in the end, peeves about bosses and glass ceilings and assorted niggling little wounds.

She opened her book and started losing herself in the safe and skirt-swishing world of *Love in the Afternoon* while continuing to lightly stroke the cat's back. After thirty pages or so, she heard Darren at the apartment door. She heard him take off his shoes to honor the light beige carpet—his color choice not hers. They exchanged hellos. When she heard him walk to the back bedroom which also housed his desk and computer, she allowed herself to dive back into her embarrassingly unintellectual but yearningly romantic book again. Rakish and uplifting banter between the two protagonists. Simple. Lovely. Enchanting. It brought a smile to her face.

"What are you reading?" Darren asked from the open doorway. She hadn't heard his socks on the soft carpet.

"A book," she said and fled with it to the bathroom. Her cheeks prickled with mortification.

Unnecessary Mountain

Spring break. Maria and Dan were out looking for Unnecessary Mountain. Both college teachers, he History, she English, they had splurged on a trip to the coast. Their daughter Belinda was in college herself now and hanging out with college friends. Maria sometimes worried about her. Dan didn't. Women did pretty well these days, he would say.

They did reach Unnecessary Mountain but didn't know this for sure until they confirmed it after their return on one of Dan's maps. There came a point at the foot of another steep incline where they simply decided to turn around and head back to the trailhead. On the way they stopped at a spectacular overlook for a picnic. Dan liked to stop for spectacular views and for picnics. Maria generally preferred to munch and take in vistas while walking. But there was no harm in stopping.

A short while further down the trail they met a heavyset young man, huffing and puffing and glistening with sweat on face and sturdy arms. His shirt was drenched. Dan liked to stop and chat with fellow hikers on trails. Maria didn't, but there was no harm in stopping for a few minutes. The men talked about this and that. The young man planned to reach the Lions. Dan wasn't sure they could be reached directly from this trail. Maria, always friendly, added: "But just a few steps further up the trail, there's a beautiful overlook where you could stop for a picnic."

Later she couldn't remember exactly what Dan said, only that it had the flavor of *this, dear, is a conversation among men.* It reminded her of the words from the Bible where Paul writes: Let your women keep silence in the congregations.

She was quiet all the way home. It would have been too difficult for her to adequately voice how small and how devastating the ache was. Like a fine cactus needle back home in the desert. Dan never noticed. Her silence often had that effect.

Miniskirt

On the first day of winter break, both their student grades finished for the term, they finally had time to shop for Christmas. Actually, her grades had been done for days. She had a system. But Kevin tended to procrastinate, and his sloppy record keeping didn't make the process any easier.

At the mall, while looking for something to send to his parents, Robin saw two gorgeous ruffled miniskirts in a store window. Three layers of ruffles. One skirt was turquoise with black polka dots, the other one was golden. She fell in love with the golden skirt. She made a huge production of how much she loved it. Even though it was just days before Christmas, since Kevin always waited until the last possible minute to buy her presents, she thought she stood a chance.

On Christmas day, there was a box from that store done up in gift paper. Things went warm in her chest, nerves were prancing around singing "yes." She opened the box. It contained the turquoise skirt. She looked at him in surprise. His face was beaming.

She tried to smile. "I'm curious," she said. "Why did you get the turquoise one and not the golden one?"

"I thought the golden one would be impractical," he said after a pause.

She would have loved that golden skirt. Now she had a turquoise miniskirt she didn't exactly mind but didn't love. And it was not one bit more practical than the golden one would have been. She didn't plan on teaching Composition 101 in her new turquoise polka dot miniskirt.

Two Minutes

9:48 a.m. So many yellow flowers down here at the river, hundreds of little suns. It is gorgeous and exactly as he described it. I won't cross the river, though I can see the trail on the other side. I did bring my wading shoes just in case, but I won't use them. I don't want to inadvertently miss him. I've already worried about missing him on the trail down, but I only stepped off the trail that once, and I kept the trail in sight all the time. In places the trail almost tricked me. At about twenty-five minutes up the drainage, it veers off to the right and climbs for quite a while instead of continuing straight down. That made me nervous.

I came early. He traditionally comes to meeting places early. I don't want him to have to wait. After five solo days in the wilderness, I want him to feel a warm welcome. He said to meet him between eleven and twelve down by the river. I brought my notebook and my pens to while away the time.

The hike down made me sweaty, so I'm sitting in the sun to dry out. It's just a bit chilly in the wind.

The drive to the trailhead parking lot was enchanting early in the morning. Orion was just fading. Everything looked fresh and filled with hope. I didn't see a bear this time like we did one dawn coming around a curve on the highway.

10:45 a.m. I'm right opposite of where he is likely to emerge from the trees. It's getting close to 11 o'clock.

11:10 a.m. He'll be here any minute now. I thought he'd have been here by now. I checked the email with his two-week itinerary again last night, just to be sure to get here at the right time. I do see where he should emerge from the other side of the river. The pale grass is high over there, and a few thousand bright yellow flowers grow over there as well. Once in a while the wind moves in the trees just so and I think it is his beige flap hat moving into sight. But no. Not yet.

I can't really focus on writing, not while also constantly looking over at the trail on the other side of the water. It's a bit like at an airport, you can't read or write, not while also keeping an eye on the passengers coming down the arrival hallway. Nerves. Anticipation. Anxiety. I will be so happy to see him.

I love the wet grass smell of the river, mixed with the surprisingly fresh scent of decaying leaves.

11:32 a.m. I'll see him any minute now. I do regret that we have somehow lost the wild desire of early days together. And so soon. I want to believe it wasn't my doing. I've done everything I could to earn love and devotion. Which can't be earned. I get that. But. I did so want to do everything in my power. Looks like I'm just not talented enough to inspire him. Or not imperious enough. Should have been a bitch perhaps. Should have let myself be chased. And I didn't.

I am only thirty-seven. I didn't expect to be jaded until much, much later on. If ever. I'm not ready yet to surrender to the dull prison of acceptance.

What worries me is that he sent a message with one of his friends before he split off for his solo adventure that I shouldn't panic if he didn't come today. There was a chance of storms, and I should let the Forest Service know approximately where on his itinerary he might be if the weather turned bad. So far, the weather has been fine.

I spent all day yesterday preparing for today. Buying ice, sandwich stuff, etc. I so want to be loved, appreciated. If he started walking at 9:00 a.m., he should get here soon. I really thought he would have been here by now. This place is spectacular, tall rock columns all around, the water gurgling gently. I saw a cottonwood leaf detach and float to the ground, then I saw another leaf dance off on the water.

I am not to worry. Okay then. I am so looking forward to his head bobbing up the trail. We haven't really made any contingency arrangements about today. It would be wonderful if he just came up the narrow path now and we could have a picnic and start walking back up the trail to the parking lot. I must remember to offer to carry some of his stuff.

I want to show him how welcome he is. Not that it matters much what I do. He always believes he is welcome anyway. Which is okay with me.

I have lots more hours of daylight.

11:51 a.m. A small boy just jolted me with his sharp cry of joy at seeing the water. A human voice after all this silence. I wish it was you. Now the boy and his parents found a shady spot and are eating lunch a little way upstream on a rock. My beautiful solitude gone for a while. It is hot now, and there's little shade here by the riverbank. I still want to be in this spot. I can see the trail on the other side of the river best from here. At least I have the shade from my ball cap. And sunscreen of course. I'll put on some more in a minute. The yellow flowers stand so tall. It's their last extravaganza of summer. The sun is making me drowsy, but I don't want to fall asleep. What if he came and didn't see me?

There, another leaf floating down. Where are you, my love, and why aren't you here yet?

Would I stay where we live if you didn't return? I'm not sure. At first, yes, of course, since I own the house. But it wasn't my choice of place. If I could live anywhere in the world, where would I go? I don't really know. Maybe the small town I visited in Italy when I was a child. Maybe some Greek island. I still have dreams, but I am also tired, even of dreaming. I don't have passion anymore. My desires have all dulled down, and I don't want dull, not in this one and only life I have. I really wanted to draw him into my world of passion. Instead, I'm being drawn into his world of practical indifference.

Almost noon already. I've been here for two hours now. Looking at the same path, the same green trees. If necessary, I'll drive home and come again tomorrow.

12:21 p.m. I want to do what's right. Part of me imagines you unexpectedly up at the parking lot already, dirty, exhausted, having missed me on the trail somehow. I don't think you have a car key with you. And me down here with all my sandwiches and sparkling water and nuts.

If we don't connect today, will I drive the two and a half hours home, or stay in a campsite at the hot springs? Probably camp.

I feel such tenderness for you. I'm suddenly convinced you won't come today.

The sun is hot in my neck. The little boy and his parents have left. I am alone again.

There, a dragonfly, blue, beautiful.

12:28 p.m. It would be best if you came in the next few minutes. I'll do a meditation now, with my eyes wide open.

12:50 p.m. Still not here yet. Should I worry?

I can't decide what to do. Is he waiting for me to come farther? Did we miscommunicate? Did he get stuck due to high water somewhere? Is he in danger? What am I supposed to do? I so wish he'd just come walking through those trees and yellow flowers.

It is too early to lose you. Just come wandering down the path now. I will wait until 1:00 o'clock and then hike back up to the trailhead.

I remember one time at the Hampton Inn—I waited for him at what I thought was a sensible place, but he decided to change plans and do something else. Thing is, he's usually early, too, not late. Did he find some other way to the parking lot? I worry about the message from his friend, if something happens "let the Forest Service know where I am."

Are you somewhere on the trail praying I would do something other than what I am doing? If I leave at 1:00 o'clock, I'll be back up before the Visitor Center closes.

Where are you? I feel so insecure. I always feel accused. It's my mother's legacy. The echo of her frequent mantra: What have I done wrong?

I really don't know what to do. Except start hiking back at 1:00 o'clock, see if he's somehow made it to the parking lot.

And what if he is somewhere farther down on the trail hoping for me to find him?

I wish you'd just come walking along. Everything is exactly the way you described it, and yet you aren't here.

Where will I go if you don't return? I'd hate it, of course, but I'd much rather you ran away with some mountain nymph rather than be stuck in some physical distress somewhere. Be well wherever you are. Come walking up the path now. Please.

Of course I worry. Do you need my help? I feel calm but lost. I still see the trees flicker in the wind, I still keep hoping that's you coming up the path. Leaves fall. Branches dance. Hummingbirds and butterflies. Come on. Come walking toward me. Step by step. I want to see you, and it's always just shadows in the trees. You've never been late. I'm not to panic until tomorrow.

I will leave here at 1:13 p.m. That's 1313 military time and 13 is my favorite number. I don't think you will come anymore. Are you lost? Did we miss each other somehow?

I don't think I would like to live without you in our house, which is really your dream house, not mine—and your dream part of the world.

It would have been lovely to meet here by the river.

What if I get to the parking lot and you're not there?

Where are you, my love? What's going on? I feel remarkably calm.

Who are we? What have we become? What is our purpose?

I hope you are well. If you could just come walking down the path, that would be fantastic.

1:13 p.m. Goodbye, beautiful river with your glittering water and your cicada song and summer sun scent.

4:12 p.m. Well, I'm back at the parking lot. He is not here. Wasn't here earlier when I came up either. I went to the Visitor Center to find out whether there was any calamity reported anywhere. Negative. And, no, they will not act on any missing hiker report until at least 48 hours have passed. I bought some yogurt and OJ at the hot springs general store. The yogurt was not very good. The Visitor Center folks recommended if it gets too stinky at the parking lot because of the horses, or too loud because of their owners, I could go to a campground a half a mile north. But I won't go just yet. Not until after dark.

So many yellow flowers up here too. Daisy types of some kind. I have to force myself to look at them. My mind keeps pulling me elsewhere. I think this is your goodbye, beautiful flowers, your yellow garlands of summer farewell.

Hiking back, I had a lot of time to think about our situation. I hope he is well. I wanted to bring him the gift of passion and instead it's turned out he's given me the dubious gift of equanimity—indifference, really—which I don't want any more than he wanted the passion I had on offer.

I am amazed that I am not frantic. As I would have been just a few years ago. There was a time, ten, twelve years ago, when I was so brilliantly in love, I would have done anything for him. I would have given my life for him. In some ways I did. I changed. It was a bit as though I died. To make his dreams possible. I flowed around him and his agenda. Like the river flows around stone. He didn't particularly notice. He accepted it as more or less his due. And then he started taking it, and me, for granted. I wish I could have done better for both of us.

I'm sitting here a few feet away from the trailhead, looking up at the path from time to time. If he still comes today, he'll come down the trail from above. He can't miss me. I can't miss him. If he comes. I'll stay here until dark, then I'll drive to the campground.

I am calm. I miss the passion in me that used to burn like fire. Indifference is contagious. Passion apparently is not. Indifference is a survival skill. Indifference is also deadly. I ache. There is a hole where my passion and my love should be. I want to be in love with this world, not trapped in this calm acceptance of things. I miss my fire.

He's told me more than once: "I do love you. Just not the way you want to be loved." But then what good is it? This is my only life. I don't want to settle for ash.

9:48 p.m. He came down the trail at 4:30 p.m. or so. I was so relieved to see him. He told me he got to the river at 1:15 p.m., two minutes after I left. Because I wasn't there, he decided to wait and see if I would still come. After an hour, he figured I wasn't coming and started to walk on up. He agreed that he had told me between eleven and twelve in his itinerary email but had then given me a different time verbally. I didn't remember that. Could be I didn't listen. A more likely story is that he believed he had told me and hadn't actually done so. We were both a little embarrassed.

We ate the sandwiches at a picnic ground off the highway on the way home. They were stale, but good enough for two hungry and tired critters. He drove all the way home. He wanted to, and I didn't. When I drive and he is the passenger, he has too many noticeable intakes of breath, though he has graciously abandoned verbal critiques.

He's asleep now in the other room, the same man he was yesterday, the same man he will be tomorrow, the same man I will always love. And yet I feel tamed into indifference. Juniper berries dropping on the roof will keep me awake for a while. And late summer cicada trill. When I fall asleep, I hope to dream of yellow flowers.

A Liar

I never thought I'd become a liar. I'm not sure if I'm any good at it. I ought to be. I've had so much practice. At night I listen to your sleep breath. Steady. Enviable. You never seem to lose sleep over anything. I didn't think I would ever lie to you. I should have known better. We're trained to lie in this world. I don't think a single culture is exempt from that. That said, I still don't know if I'm any good at it.

There've been so many times I was bubbly and happy, until I told you whatever it was that made me sing. You have this way of smoothing, nay smothering, the fire out of the enthusiasm. Then I feel like a little girl asking for attention, being reminded it's not good to be too boisterous in public. Not good indeed. Subdued is more acceptable. Though then I feel like the middle-aged woman I am. Only more so. I still want to be a breathtaking princess. Instead, I feel like Edith Bunker on a dreary winter day.

I don't remember exactly when I started lying to you. The other lying started way back when. Must never say what you see when you look at your father. Unless it's something wonderful. If necessary, lie and make him feel good. Your brothers? You could get away with the truth, but it's not recommended. And God? Well, He's in a category all of His own. And, no, God is never mean, not even when He allows children to be killed in war or famine and then won't even admit them to paradise unless they are baptized, which often they aren't because nobody where they lived even knows about that rule.

Like most couples, we've been through so many variations of "What's wrong?" "Nothing." "Sure?" "Yeah." And the problem is, if I do open up, I'm in danger of getting a platter of platitudes. And who wants that? So, no excessive exuberance. Wasn't there a line in a movie about that? And no whining about anything, getting another shared sunset off the to do list, for instance, or endlessly cheery dinner conversations, not enough roses, too many unnecessary chores, no illusions of being important, this lackluster limping along side by side, while still unsuccessfully nursing the wish to be your dream woman. On occasion you tell me how happy I am, and I don't know what you are talking about.

Sometimes I wish I were back in a time when I didn't have to lie, when my love for you was a sparkling fountain of devotion. A time when we could tell each other everything. Well, I don't know about you. I could tell you everything, without fear of being judged. I was that breathtaking then. I really was, wasn't I?

Anyway, fairy tales are always more profitable than exact reality. Priests. Ministers. Politicians. All with their preferred fairy tales. Even the medical profession. Do this and that, and all will be well. And then that awful New Age insinuation that you bring physical trauma on yourself by not having the proper attitude. So, where did I go wrong here, God, universe, spirit, whoever you are? I went to the doctor today at lunch to discuss the results. She estimates I have two to fifteen months left, and the pain will likely increase in short order, so I won't be able to keep it under wraps much longer. I mean, with all that lying and secret-keeping and so forth, how am I supposed to tell you that I'll likely not be here—at least not in my physical manifestation—fifteen months from now, maybe sooner?

There, I hear your key in the door.

"Howdy, Mel." I hear you plunk your daypack on the hall table. "How was your day?"

"Fine. Yours?"

"Good. Anything happening?" You breeze into the kitchen, fresh autumn air from your brisk walk home still clings to your jacket.

"No. Just the usual." In a way that's almost even the truth. I've been lying for so long. Then one more lie qualifies as usual, doesn't it?

"Something smells good," you say.

Seven Years

What were the happiest years of my life? That's easy. It was those seven years I was engaged to your father. As you probably remember, I was nineteen when I met him. I was smitten. He was too. Then we got secretly engaged. And that's when the romance started. Your grandfather was not impressed when they first met. He called Willy a vagabond. But Willy had only taken off a year to travel, to see something of the world. At times he traveled with a friend, other times on his own. Your grandmother liked him better, presumably because he had good manners, and he knew how to flatter her. He stayed at our farm for three weeks in October, helping with the potato crop and taking care of the cows. He would have stayed longer, but Father decided he didn't have any more work for a traveling fellow. Which was not true; he simply wanted to get Willy off the farm because it was pretty obvious how taken I was. So, Willy moved on. He kept taking all kinds of odd jobs and stayed in many different places. Almost everywhere else he was more welcome than at our farm. He wanted to see different places, however, and so he kept on moving.

He promised to write to me, and he did. Because I didn't want your grandfather to know how many letters I was getting, I had Willy address his letters to the post office in the next town over. I'd bicycle there once or twice a week, and there was almost always a new letter, sometimes even two. I'm not sure you can do this anymore these days, but back then it was possible. I could write to him the same way, to whatever town he thought he was going to be next. I was convinced that I kept all this a big secret from your grandfather, though nowadays I'm not so sure. He probably knew all along. I mean, word does get around, and if a young woman from a neighboring town comes all the time to pick up mail, it's probably common gossip. But I believed I was safe in my private dealings, and I could dream a future with

Willy to my heart's content.

And did I ever dream! Our future was going to be wonderful. When he went back to studying, he too had a fixed address again, and we could now write to each other regularly. Sort of like kids today write each other emails. Or texts. Our often daily letters were longer than your typical email or text, however, and they were full of plans. I thrived on the intensity of those dreamy letters. He was going to finish his studies and as soon as he could afford to, he would ask your grandfather for my hand and then marry me. We were going to make love at least once a day, have at least four children, and live a fairy tale life.

Instead, the war started. I wanted to marry him before he had to go, and this time your grandfather relented, after listening to my probably unnecessary confession that we'd been corresponding for the last seven years which proved that we were in a serious and lasting relationship. And we were. When Willy passed away, we had been married for fifty-four years. They were good years, and we were both grateful for everything that came our way, including you four children. But the magic of those seven years of waiting for each other never returned. Now instead of poetry and over the moon declarations of love, we bravely lived side by side discussing radishes for his supper sandwiches and bananas for breakfast. I suppose there is some poetry in fifty-four years of radishes, but it doesn't quite amount to the kind of adoration I had been looking forward to. Maybe, too, I was simply more attractive on paper. I did miss the sweetness of the letter writing years, the spirit years. I remember. All my best love was conducted long-distance. The fifty-four years of reality tended to be more draining, and I was never very good at reality. Dreaming was easier.

A Walk by the Ocean

The kids are safely parked in college. On scholarships. There's even money in the bank in case the scholarships don't cover everything. The freezer is filled. Dean wouldn't starve until we all figure out what's what. Today I could make it to Yuma or Calexico. Tomorrow I could be walking by the ocean somewhere. I yearn for the ocean, its majesty. I yearn for time to hurl myself like a tall wave against this lifelong acceptance of what comes shimmeringly close to indifference.

I was raised with ten-thousand mandates for modesty. Like a strange fish, I feel stranded by rules I have followed, locked in this invisible soft prison of respectability. I could just get into the car and start driving. Instead, I lie next to Dean, unable to sleep, cradling our fragile love in my arms, afraid to let go, not sure of the cost if I did let go, and above all too tired to run away, and ironically too tired even to fall asleep.

He is a good man. And then again, I am a good woman, too. Only, he is—what's that lamentable phrase again? Not into me. That's it. And I am slowly but surely and unwillingly drifting into an indifference of my own. We're both yearning for something that seems to be beyond our reach. I wonder what his dreams are. He doesn't say. Heck, I don't even know what *my* dreams are besides wanting to walk by the ocean.

I am so tired of spending most of my nights trying to fall asleep. As soon as my exhausted head hits the pillow, I am wide awake, yearning for deliverance from this gentle prison.

I might only make it as far as Phoenix. There's a rest area on I-8, not too far beyond Phoenix, where I could sleep for a while, then resume my escape. I am afraid, though, I'll never outrun this chronic tiredness.

And if I ran away for good, how would I support

myself? I have no idea. Maybe I'd get a job as a checkout clerk at some store. I'm old enough now to even be able to work as a waitress. Nobody is likely anymore to pinch my butt. Though you never know. There seems to be no limit to the general lust for putting women in their place. Which makes me even more exhausted. How many years have I had to try and hold up my head in the face of all these subtle, mostly inadvertent methods of belittlement? Too many, that's what. Far too many. At any rate, at this point I am too tired to run away. Perhaps I'm simply too old to run away.

Letting my mind do the wandering is easier anyway. No mosquitoes, no scorpions, no growling dogs, no alarming strangers following too close for comfort.

I listen to Dean's breath and want to shelter him in any way I can. He turns in his sleep and puts his arm across my ribcage. When I close my eyes, I can feel the fierce damp wind from the ocean bring tears.

Under the Bridge: A Letter Home

Dear Kevin,

I made it to Denver this week. Gorgeous sunlight. Not too warm.

Under the bridge by the Platte River, I keep seeing the same woman, eyes stern, severe, a little wounded, looking at me with sullen challenge. Who are you? Leave me alone. Looking for trouble? Don't bother me. I'm tired of y'all. Today when I passed, she pulled her cover, a thin yellow and brown blanket, closer to her face. This slid the blanket away from her feet, clad in heavy brown ankle boots, scuffed. The toe of the right boot sported a huge hole. Her legs lay side by side straight out in front of her like sticks as her back leaned upright against the wall. A swag of ivy hung over her head. Her eyes were dark with suspicion, almost black. They moved from me to the shopping cart on her side. Back to me, back to the cart. She peered behind it too once, as though defending it with her meticulous attention. It was a large shopping cart from the nearby supermarket, piled high with things hidden under a black plastic sheet.

Today was the third day I saw her sit in the exact same spot, looking at me with the same brooding eyes, guarding the same heaping cart with its black plastic sheet concealing things of significance to her. Somehow she had to be getting food. Did she ever leave her spot? With or without her cart? Does someone come to bring her food and drink and company? I wonder what her dreams are as she sits there with her eyes on the river, leaning against stone under ivy, held captive by what she owns.

You too have many treasures. I know they are important to you.

I miss you so much. Be well. I will not come home again.

Conspiracy Theory

"It's not that I don't like sex. I just don't like it in literature," she declared, working her ostrich feather fan. A few heads turned. A few jaws dropped and one wine glass.

That night she dreamed.

Men in pale blue and white shirts sat around a mahogany board room table. Some had their sleeves rolled up. Dark suit jackets lay on the table or rested slung across the backs of cushioned chairs. Not a woman in sight. The only women in evidence were the subject matter of their stimulating discussion. These women were all literate now. Almost all of them liked romances, with the exception of a few who had been meticulously shamed out of that partiality at the same time and with the same tools as they had been shamed out of everything else labeled sentimental in the course of a preemptive intellectual education. Another very few were simply not romantically inclined.

How to proceed? The publishing world still needed these women's lucrative devotion, but it wouldn't do to surrender the world to women's sentiments.

One man in a blue and white striped shirt came up with a brilliant idea.

"While we like girls in their summer dresses," he said, "as well as ladies barefoot on swings, or barefoot anywhere else for that matter, let's face it: we like sex even better. So, let's insert mandatory sex scenes into their romances. Furthermore, let's tell them they're the ones asking for it. No, never mind asking. We'll tell them they are clamoring for it. Let them have their swaggering devoted heroes, but the price will be sex. Just as it is and should be in real life."

"Great idea, Tom," said another. "Let's run a market study pronto to back up our claims."

"No market study, Dick," said a third dismissively. "We're not running this by the women. We'll tell them what they like. We've always done that. We're good at it."

"Sounds more like a punishment than a fair price, Harry," said Dick. "Especially without asking the ladies first."

"Ask, shmask," Harry said.

"That's right," Tom said, colluding in hushing Dick's thoughtful concern. "It's our world. We make the rules. If somebody, especially a man, writes an intellectual or literary tome, then sex can still be optional. But if someone wants to write something that is strictly for a woman's fantasy market, we have a perfect right to add a little indoctrination. Sex is good. All women worth their salt should be capable of earthquaking pleasure. With the right shaft, the right core, and the right seed everything falls into place. Amen."

"Do you really think it will fly?" Dick was still skeptical. "For five thousand years we've been able to manage with sexless literature, and we've managed pretty well. Give or take a few hush-hush pornographic items, we've gotten by sexless pretty much until D. H. Lawrence and Henry Miller and their ilk. And now you want to have not just optional but obligatory sex when women write for women?"

"It'll fly," Harry said. "Trust me. It'll fly. That's what the sexual revolution was for. Why not take advantage of it?"

"Let me play devil's advocate. Or angel's advocate, if you will. What if they really don't like it?"

"No worries. They will. Remember, we will have told them they like it. We will have told them what they want. Besides, it is only right. If we allow them their impossibly gentle and generous and chivalrous heroes, who are making all the rest of us look bad, they will have to give us something."

Tom tittered. "I can just picture Grandma Tildy steepling her hands in astonishment, reading half a paragraph of swords and sheaths and seeds and shafts dancing around tremulous cores, then skipping over the rest of that chapter until things start looking reasonably safe again. I can imagine, too, one fine day she'll return to one of the fairy tale romances of her less explicit youth. It will comfort her. She'll read and read with stars in her eyes. But suddenly it will occur to her. 'There's something missing here.' He-he."

"Do stop tittering, Tom. It doesn't become you."

"I'm still not sure that we can just shove it down their deep throats," Dick said, with a gleam in his eyes as his ears turned pink.

"Oh, stop it, Dick," said Harry. "Do you want to set off Tom again?"

It was too late. Tom was quaking with amusement, as were the dozen or so interns in attendance who had not spoken up but had followed the debate with blushing interest.

"Seriously," Harry said. "It's not betrayal. It's simply win win in our favor. Like friends with benefits. Now romances with sex. It's good to be alive."

"Hear, hear," he heard.

"That's settled then," Harry said, expanding his chest to where his shirt buttons could barely contain it. He glanced around the table, collecting roguish and unanimous nods.

And this is how it came about that all romances now have obligatory sex in them, while for the remainder of the literary world, sex is optional.

She rubbed her eyes, delighted to wake up. Just a dream, she tried to comfort herself. Just a dream.

Dear Connor

This is the last letter I will not send.

Last week I was still full of blossoms for you. I rode up on the elevator with a man who reminded me of you. How beautiful you were. Irish in part, said the man on the elevator. He said his mother's name was Murphy. He marveled how he had never seen me before. I've been here all the time.

I saw him three times. Then not again. The third time, I walked behind him. He was limping, badly.

Connor, for twenty-three years I loved you. I was entranced by the beauty of your being. The wildness, the seriousness, and, I have to confess, the suffering, too. You guys do that to attract us, don't you? Put on the suffering act. But once we are attracted, strangely enough you turn away. You choose the ones who don't care. I guess this keeps your suffering intact.

The Christmas card I sent you came back. I am glad. I loved you so much. You and your many women. You always loved the ones who did not care.

You made me believe I was not beautiful, not as interesting as the others, those mysterious, distant, unattainable ones. It never occurred to me till now how wrong you were. I am beautiful. Very much so. I always was. Why did you never see my beauty? Why were you cold? Because I loved you?

I know you didn't want the happiness on offer.

You have colored my life. I thought I was a mouse, a Cinderella of no consequence. I thought I would never amount to anything, because you didn't seem to think I would ever amount to anything.

How awkwardly we choose our loves. I, too, was looking to the wrong one. You.

I wanted to be loved like you loved Lily. With total longing and abandon. I remember sitting with her at the bottom of the staircase, talking of oranges and immortality. You came along and claimed her to bed, and she went.

Shortly after that, she left for good. She was probably bored with your whiskey-drenched, soul-searching aches and your Weltschmerz.

Mostly, I guess, I too loved my own longing, for the beauty in you that wasn't entirely real. Handsome? Yes. Tall, strong, rugged, well-proportioned. Nice hair. But your eyes were small, and too often blood-shot. And lots of pock marks in your face.

How I was humbled by loving you. I am still surprised at how beautiful I am and how I still don't believe it. I look in the mirror. I shine. But if I am so beautiful now, I was certainly even more beautiful twenty-three years ago. And if I was so beautiful then, how could you not have loved me?

I walked around campus dreaming of you. How you would touch me, love me. How we would stand together in the sun of spring, your tall head bent low. I loved you so much, dear Connor. Why could you not love me?

I saw you dance once at a party at some professor's house. I wanted to dance with you. You never asked. I have come a long way. These days I dance by myself.

I have spent twenty-three years doing the most fascinating things without you.

This is my year of learning how to parallel park. This is my year of learning how to let go of you.

Dear John

I saw something in your eyes tonight. It said *if you asked me, my dear, I would stay with you.*

I can't ask that.

You see, once upon a time I had a friend. She had large freckles in a narrow face and her stringy blond hair was always tied up in a lanky ponytail. She wore conservative skirts. And I loved her. To me she was beautiful. On school days, I would pick her up from her apartment building each morning, her mom waving down to us from their second story bay window. We rode the tram together. Then we would sit side by side in our classroom all day long while teachers came and went. We ate our snacks together, yogurt or milk, a homemade sandwich perhaps, and from time to time a nut and honey pastry. We were inseparable. When fellow students or teachers invited either one of us to an extra-curricular event, they would as a matter of course invite the other one, too. She refused to go to parties, though, so I attended those on my own. When we were sixteen, I went away as an exchange student for a year. It was marvelous.

The following year when school started again, I took my old seat next to her. She stopped by our two-seater desk to solemnly tell me that, in my absence, she had made a new friend and wanted to now go sit with her. I looked up and saw her new best friend watch us from a short distance away.

"But you are *my* friend," I said. "You can't just leave me."

I don't remember what all we said that day. Did I say, *no, you are mine?* I must have been persuasive, for she stayed with me, and I watched her wanting to be elsewhere all year long. I got what I asked for. It was no good. It wasn't what I wanted. I sensed her loyal regret, and then my own regret for having asked for more than what was on offer. It would have been better to let her go.

Our time together was splendid, John. Go now. Let's not overstay desire while it turns into a sad limp of questionable triumph.

In the end, we all live lovely lives anyway.

My Brother's Bride

I've watched him all my life. He's my brother. I know all about him, what color Easter eggs he prefers, what instrument he likes to play most, and how he first fell in love with Tammy. Carlos made falling in love feel like the world was suddenly one endless song. He sang it in his room; he sang it at the dinner table; he sang it giving me a ride to school. I was only fourteen then. He was twenty-one. Tammy was the love of his life, and I was spell-bound. As far as I was concerned, she walked on water. As did he, of course. Carlos wrote songs for her. Some of them are still being played on the radio. And they still get a gazillion of views on YouTube. He wanted to take her to Paris for her own twenty-first birthday, but she said no. He got her a puppy instead. That she accepted, and she loved the puppy. Her birth name was Tamar, but she preferred Tammy. I would have preferred that, too.

She was beautiful then. Still is. So was he. Then. And now too, even as he is balding on top and putting on some weight around the middle. He wanted to marry her, of course. I don't know why she said no. I would have married him myself if I wasn't his sister. He didn't give up for a very long time. When she was married to some guy from her family's circle of friends at twenty-four, Carlos stayed in the background. When she divorced at twenty-five because her husband was unfaithful to her, though that was customary in their culture, Carlos was right there, a shoulder to cry on, a friend to hug, a man to reassure her that she hadn't lost any of her allure. And of course, he was still hoping it would lead to more. She went out with him, they had long all-night conversations, he often stayed at her apartment, and she came to dinner at our house on Sundays. When she wasn't available, he spent many night hours talking to me about his tender dreams for a common future as well, and I gave him whatever advice and encouragement a kid sister could give. It looked promising. And still she said no when he asked her once again to marry him. I never understood. I should have been angry with her, and I couldn't even manage that. No one can stay angry with her for longer than a minute. She's that kind of magical creature.

A few years down the road, she married another guy, another one I couldn't figure out what on earth she saw in him when she could have had my amazing brother. The second guy she married was completely ordinary. He worked as a store manager in a grocery store. He sure didn't write songs for her. Her first husband at least wrote a few poems in his spare time. Her second husband? No such thing. Carlos went to their wedding. I was invited too, but I didn't go. In her late thirties, Tammy had two kids, cementing her marriage to Mr. Ordinary. I think that's when Carlos gave up on his devotion. Tired of hopelessness, I suppose. I didn't blame him. He dated lots and lots of women, like a series of auditions. Women were always attracted to him because of his music and his glamor and his fame. All except the elusive Tammy.

One fine day he decided to settle down. Selena is lovely enough. When he asked her to marry him, of course she said yes. We all went to Italy for the wedding, rented a castle, complete with a small lake, and I was the wedding photographer.

I am looking at the photos now. There is Selena in her long white dress with a veil with a long lacy train that two girls carried as she walked down the aisle. A fairytale princess. Knowing Carlos, I imagine he promised himself that Selena will never know that his heart was still elsewhere, burning like a solitary candle in some side-chapel of an ancient cathedral. He probably left the hymnal open on the altar but closed the door to the chapel forever. One day, I'm sure, Selena will look at all these photos I took and be filled with nostalgia. By the lake. On the castle wall. In the rose garden. At twilight under a tree with an owl looking down on them. One of the photos grates on me. Carlos is bent from the waist, kissing her hand which she imperiously holds out to him. They look both serious and slightly mocking at one and the same time. Maybe truth is like that. Serious and mocking. I don't know. It looks so romantic and so wrong because I know his heart still flutters elsewhere. It's a heavy secret. I hope Selena and I never have a falling out. I'd be afraid of spilling the beans that Carlos has been careful not to spill. How he gave his heart that once, and it was never returned. Yes, of course Selena knows that once upon a time he dated the beautiful Tammy, but she has no clue how deep that love went as far as Carlos was concerned. I wonder if Tammy ever looks at Carlos and Selena from a safe distance—it wouldn't be difficult, the two of them are always in the news—regretting what could have been. Sometimes at night I feel like crying for him. Or for myself. I wish someone would love me the way he loved Tammy, or that I would find someone to love from my end the way he loved Tammy. One needs to be so brave in this incomprehensible world.

Mark and Martina

Mark was the breadwinner, an attorney. Martina was the dancer. It suited them well. He had great stage presence in front of the jury, blond, handsome, suave. She twirled in the kitchen, on the living room parquet floor; she danced with their two children, Haley and Tim, and sent them to ballet school. Both children liked it, and she was pleased. Martina was lovely but also strict with the children and she kept a wonderful house. From time to time, she regretted that she didn't get as much spotlight in life as she would have liked. Mark kept his thick blond hair way into his forties, with a longish lock over his forehead that he had actually practiced tossing in front of the bathroom mirror for alluring effect. Martina kept her slender figure, despite the gourmet meals she cooked. The children were proud of their mom because she was graceful and smart. They were proud of both their parents, really. Mark was the easier parent, cuddly and permissive when he was not annihilating his opponents in front of a riveted jury. At home Martina was the bossy one, though, so it seemed to count more when the children were able to impress her.

The one thing missing from Martina's life was dancing, real dancing, not just cavorting with the children. Mark claimed he was simply too clumsy and couldn't understand rhythm. On rare occasions they swayed on the local dance floor to slow music in close embrace. It wasn't very satisfying. In her family there had always been a lot of dancing and they all danced well. Ricardo, Pablo, Fernando. Sometimes they danced with her in a club, but dancing with her own brothers wasn't exactly satisfying either. Besides, more often than not they were dancing with their own wives.

As defense attorney, Mark occasionally had trouble collecting fees and ended up doing *pro bono* work. It wasn't that big a deal. He still made a more than comfortable living for all of them. One time, defending a young woman successfully on a spurious assault charge, she tearfully declared she had no money left to pay the remainder of her fee when the victorious verdict came in. Her sister, in attendance for the celebration, had no money either, but she ran a dance studio and offered to give Mark and Martina dance lessons to work off what her sister still owed.

"No, it's not our thing," Mark said. But then he saw Martina's eyes, filled with longing. "Actually, maybe we could try," he said.

Martina's face glowed with pleasure.

They signed up for a sampler series of ballroom dances. In class he was clumsy at first, as he had expected all along. Waltz wasn't for him. Rumba was a little better. Merengue was easy, but it didn't inspire him. And then tango happened. It was his dance. He could be flamboyant. He could be dramatic. He could be masterful. Martina was ecstatic. This was how it should have been all along.

The teacher complimented him. Their fellow students adored him. He was in his element. He was willing to dance this dance for the rest of his life. Maybe go to tango conventions. There seemed to be so many all over the country. Maybe go study in Argentina. Why not? Or Europe. Paris, he learned, had been a hotbed for expatriate *tangueros* in the early days.

Soon when it came to lady's choice, he was swarmed by eager partners. Soon Martina was sitting out dance after dance while he was being courted and clearly enjoying himself.

For Valentine's Day he bought the family tickets to Buenos Aires for next summer's vacation. He told the children but asked them to keep it a secret from their mother until the day came. All three of them were excited.

Meanwhile he wanted to take some private lessons. During their first private lesson he noticed that Martina was quiet, irritated, it seemed. Must have had a bad day. He'd ask her about it later. The teacher kept praising him, though, and it warmed his heart. How far he had come, finally granting Martina's wish to have a dancer of her own in her life.

Martina hedged about scheduling their next lesson. She had too many other appointments the following week, and apparently the week after as well. They finally left it that they would call.

He knew something was wrong but couldn't figure out what it was.

"You've been quiet," he said. "What's wrong?"

"I just think we are getting a bit too old to dance," she said.

He wanted to protest. But suddenly he understood. She was supposed to be the dancer in the family.

He changed the tickets. The family went to Athens that summer, one of the cradles of Western civilization. The children never said a word about the change of venue.

Lovers or Not

She writes we had been lovers that year. That makes me feel exposed. It's not how I remember it.

I asked for her definition of lovers. She described stuff that would certainly qualify, even in my definition, but it was stuff we never did. How is it possible to live in such different realities?

Yes, she did visit me one weekend. And she was on the phone with her jealous girlfriend practically the whole time, at lunch, at supper, at two or three in the morning, again at four o'clock, then at breakfast. She had in fact come to visit me precisely to make her girlfriend jealous, and it worked. If she sacrificed me to propitiate her wobbly girlfriend, they would miraculously get back together. It seemed to work well for a short while of passion, but in the long run, it turned out I was sacrificed in vain.

Oh, I do remember being in love with her. I remember yearning for her, and still I nobly sent her back to her demanding and now properly jealous girlfriend. Surely if we had made love in addition to my bittersweet yearning, I would remember that? Instead, I remember sitting on the swings by the landfill after she had left, daydreaming of my own nobility in telling her to go where she really wanted to be.

Now she tries to shame me into admitting that we did make love by writing, "If you don't remember, then I guess I wasn't very memorable." Hint, hint, please stroke and save my ego here.

I wasn't mad at her back then. But now I am mad. And worried as well. I want to remember my past my way.

It scares me, too. How many others are out there wandering the face of the earth believing they have made love with me when my reality protests otherwise?

The System

Had a problem with the system today. Our tech guy is on vacation, so they send Robert, the IT guy from the Dean's office.

At first, I'm happy. I've always liked him. Even though he requires attention while he's working. He's brilliant at what he does. But he does like to talk. I can't do anything else while he's working on my computer. When he's run out of technical stuff to talk about, half of which I don't follow in the first place, he talks about anything at all.

He knows that I love to dance. I have two posters of tango dancers on my desk.

"That you and Kevin?" he asks.

"I wish. Kevin won't dance."

"Looks like you," he says. Then he tells me how he used to like dancing. "Slow dances, you know. But then it occurred to me: Why should I dance just to please a woman?"

He doesn't even notice how quiet I have become.

Lee's Story

The trouble is, I like Patrick's wife almost as much as I like Patrick. Boy, can he be weird. Crass. And when he drinks too much, forget it. But basically, he's caring and, well, cool. And she? She's weird, too. Elusive. You try to touch her, grab, hold on to her, and she just sort of slithers away, physically and intellectually.

For one thing, she's not quite as smart as she thinks she is, no matter how much she knows.

I wish my name weren't Angelina. I mean, can you beat that for sappy? Gag-a-maggot. What did they have in mind? A little princess? Thumbelina? I'm five nine and a healthy young giant, thank you very much. Yes, giant. Not giantess. I'm as good as any man. But so long as they call me Lee, I guess I can live with that.

So, I'm supposed to be incredibly excited about being twenty-one. Matter of fact, everything makes me feel horrible and itchy. I hate it when anybody says, "happy birthday" anymore, or "happy new year," "happy anything." I'd like to know what's supposed to be so happy about any of it. It'll just be one day after another, and each one of them worse than the one before. I know. I've been here. For all of twenty-one of these allegedly exciting units. Wish I'd stayed eighteen. Six or seven wasn't all that bad either. Twenty-one is the pits. No wonder they let you buy drinks. You need them!

Anyway, I am in love with Patrick because he admires my paintings. And in a way, what we do in art class is the closest to what's me, personally, whatever that is.

He's straight out of *Narcissus and Goldmund*. He loves everybody. Every woman.

His wife?

I don't know if he loves her or not.

If I were her, I wouldn't let him out of my sight.

She's the better artist, though. Her paintings are clear.

Radiant. And of course, they hang all over the place. But as a person, she's a shadow.

I hate it, though, when the other girls in class joke about her. "She's just jealous 'cause he's so popular, especially with us ladies." Giggle. Giggle. Gigolo.

In reality she's wonderful. They just don't know that. Every time I go to their house, she is warm. Interesting, too. Fascinating, really. Only thing is, she doesn't know I'm making love with her husband. It's okay, because I can handle it. Much better than anyone else could. You see, Elena, I don't want to take your husband away. Not really. I just want to make him feel better.

It simply happened. I was standing there with my turpentine rag, my hands busy and filled with muck. He brushed a strand of my hair back behind my ear, and then he kissed me.

"I'm sorry. I couldn't help it," he said.

What was I supposed to do, I'd like to know? Pour turpentine on him? For making me feel wonderful? So, I told him he didn't have to be sorry.

"But yes, I do," he said. "I don't have the right to kiss anyone as lovely as you."

"Don't you all the time?" I teased him. "Considering how lovely your wife is?" It's true—she's far more beautiful than mousy me, even though she's around fifty. Well, I'm not exactly mousy. I merely have some sort of rabbit face compared to hers. And rabbits aren't ugly, either. It's just that she…she sparkles. Anyway, I teased him, but I didn't feel a lot of levity inside. In fact, I felt quite heavy. And I wanted to cover up for it by laughing.

I sure don't want to hurt anybody.

I remember his response to what I said.

"Ah, yes," he said, like a snail withdrawing into its shell. "The beautiful Elena."

She doesn't make him happy.

"Well, I don't make her very happy either," he said. At least he's fair. "I'm just a failure as a man, I guess."

"You don't look like a failure to me," I said, touching

his face.

He gave me a crooked smile. "That's what you think. I am. You are just being kind."

"I'm not," I said. "Truly. I think you're wonderful."

"Am not."

"Are too."

Like kids.

"You're sweet," he said.

Sometimes he scares me, though. Like when he tells me that he made her cry. He said it that time because I was upset about one of the low grades she gave me.

"She doesn't count," he said. Probably wanted to reassure me. "She's nothing special. Besides, I made her cry this morning."

Ooh, I didn't like that. I suppose he wanted to show me he was on my side. But making a woman cry? Making his wife cry? And then reporting that to another woman? Scary! And she does count. To him she should count especially. He should love her. And if he can't love her all out with goo-goo eyes, then he should at least speak respectfully of her. Or else leave. No man should speak dismissively about any woman, much less his wife.

Sure, I was hurt by her remarks and by her grade. But she's still the better teacher of the two of them. Just not as much fun. It's not just that she's got the better credentials, or in fact the only real credentials of the two of them. There's more to her. It's as though she's worked on her soul more and you can almost touch it. There's something shining in her, all the way through her shadows.

But in another sense, he's the better person after all.

He's got charisma. You always want to do things for him.

You wouldn't particularly want to do things for her. You get the feeling she doesn't need you. You wouldn't dream of doing her a favor.

I was working on my green painting of the statue today, and when he came by, he said, "This is just awesome." It made me feel special. Later she came by, and she said,

"Good work there. You might want to get a little more distinct with this line here on the left."

Dr. Elena McGee, I thought. Little Dr. McGee, you've just put a pin in my balloon. I wish I could have lived with his untarnished admiration a little longer.

But he's like that, I guess. I notice how the other girls gloat when he's complimenting them. And that hurts me. I guess it's tough to share him with anyone.

It can't be easy for her.

Lucille

There was a time when I had four beautiful daughters and no importance. I loved Mark, and I was powerless. He was busy, successful, charming, and popular. When he came home from his days at the office, the girls, egged on by me, would compete at winding themselves around his legs until everybody collapsed together on the sofa for a love festival. Except me. I was the bread and butter, the everyday, the all-day-long. He was the luxury. Oh, they liked me of course, and they depended on me. I was, after all, the provider of mundane needs. They also didn't like me. Even then. I was the one who said no too often for their taste, the one who took them to the dentist and made them put on clean underwear even though that took an extra effort in the excitement of starting a new day. They didn't like that at all.

Mark was a magical father. Bell, Liz, Mia, and Jas would continue to find chocolate Easter eggs in obscure places around the house until way into July. He got all the credit of course. And he deserved most of it. He was always a lot of fun. Then again, working as a corporate attorney all day and then entertaining four boisterously happy daughters at night took its toll. He had mastered the lesson that you should not ever take out your work frustration on your children. He may have missed the lesson that recommended you do the same for your stay-at-home wife. So, when things came to a boiling point, he'd snap at me from time to time. I could even understand that.

One of the hardest things for me was to not snap back at him. Raising four daughters had its own set of frustrations. We had agreed that I would stay at home until Jas, the youngest, was in school. I had some inkling that it would be hard to be a homemaker and mom after my own brief flirtation with a career, and I was prepared to make concessions. But I wasn't prepared to become completely insignificant.

Mark and I had met in law school. We were sparkling companions, both of us ambitious, attractive, bright, friendly—the perfect couple, proving that you could have it all. As homemaker mom, I missed that. Suddenly my brains felt as though they were melting, fading, shrinking. I remembered how exuberant I had once been studying for my bar exam even while my next-door neighbor's wind chimes kept chiming in the irritating wind. Oh, I was lovely then. And excited. And exciting. Now I was a stressed mom, getting just a wee bit tired of *Make Way for Ducklings* and "Row, Row, Row Your Boat" and sewing Halloween costumes.

Instead of taking it out on Mark, I fell in love. Alex was in a vaguely similar situation. He was a free-lance writer just beginning to get published in glossy magazines, though his income was sporadic. His wife had the steady job as human resources manager in a burgeoning telecom-munications company. It was only natural that he stayed at home with their two kids, Matt and Gabe. He dispensed baby aspirins, wiped noses, did laundry, cooked hot dogs. Like me, he was often judged inadequate and irritating, and above all unimportant.

We knew each other in passing from the school parking lot, from picking up kids from co-ed soccer games, from parent teacher meetings, volunteer sessions, and so on, and it was while waiting in front of the principal's office for a dressing-down because my Bell and his Matt had participated in the organization of a stupid prank that we first felt a spark between us. Shared mortification grew into shared laughter and then into hunger. Here was an attractive member of the opposite gender that didn't see me merely as a resource, a dependable convenience. When he looked at me, there was wonder in his eyes.

At first, we kept our affair apologetically secret—we were, after all, both basically decent and loyal human beings who were not out to rock any boats or hurt our families. However, we soon found out that we were both starved for affection, for approval, for admiration, and we found that we could feed each other's hunger. And so we did. He noticed the curve of my earlobes, the sunrays in my soul, the circus of longing in my hands. Eventually we decided we really liked the feast we provided for one another, and we deserved it. Jas and his younger son, Gabe, started school the same year. And we ran away together. All the way from Colorado to Arizona. I got a job in a law office immediately, and he had more and more success with his freelance writing. We lived frugally and we were happy. We both sent home money for childcare.

Mark was devastated. People who had known us as a couple thought I was plain stupid. Such a nice guy. How could I? My daughters were even madder at me than in the old days when I had merely been a mildly burdensome presence thwarting some of their most extravagant schemes. Both Alex and I filed for divorce. Mark agreed. Alex's wife did not. Still, we lived together in beautiful Arizona, hiked in the marvels of the Grand Canyon, and lay in each other's arms until our insignificance went into remission.

It lasted a glorious year. Alex's wife ultimately prevailed, and he returned to her. He was reluctant to abandon our fairy tale, but he realized he was deep down a family man and had already once committed himself to his original family, and that was that. I wished him well. I can imagine the gossip surrounding me and Mark. "And she didn't even stay with the other guy. It barely lasted a year. He'll never take her back. I wouldn't." And Mark didn't. I knew he wouldn't, so I didn't even try.

Two years after I left, Mark married his secretary, and she was happy to be a mom to his daughters as they entered their teens one by one. He grudgingly let me spend time with our girls in their summer vacations. They gradually came to love me again and even came to understand what they had first experienced only as desertion. I hope they will have it easier. Our world being what it is, I am skeptical.

I am happy. I am alone. We all thrive on the nectar of attention, but we can exist without it. At times I listen to

"Lucille" and similar songs on my iPod, songs that remind me I was born into a world where men above all respect and honor one another. A woman who looks for pleasure or importance for herself is out of order and out of luck. All things considered, I have done well for myself. Sometimes I wonder how each of my daughters would tell this story.

I miss my illusions, but I have four beautiful daughters, and I am important.

Here on the Balcony

The waves of the Adriatic Sea look so gentle this early morning. The daily assembly of beach chairs and umbrellas hasn't been set up yet. The sand looks pristine. I wish I could own a moment like this forever. The red sun rises, the silhouette of a sailboat slowly crosses the disk of light, a shimmering path of light aims directly at me on the calm water. No one can take this away from me, not this cool morning breeze, not my long yellow silk dress fluttering against my legs. Might as well dress like a princess. Martin treats me like one. It is all like a dream. Why is it then that I cannot seem to relax? Maybe in time I will. I wish I could inhale all this deep into me to where my own sun would glow, red and golden. Instead, I feel like a stranger in my own skin, though the hair on my arms tingles as though in answer to a caress. The breeze is cooler than I expected.

We spent the first week of our marriage in a castle at the foot of the Dolomites. Martin brought me fresh flowers every day. We spent the evenings holding hands, then touching and talking by candlelight and the glow from the fireplace. Even in May, the nights were surprisingly cool. Here too. I can tell he wants to make me happy, and he does. All this is more than I have ever asked for, and yet I can't quite own it. I don't trust it. The princess makes good. And she cannot believe she is good enough to deserve it. The memories of humiliation seem more real. The gossip. The sadness.

Jeff didn't die in my arms. He died from a heart attack after a fancy dinner his parents gave at their fancy house. He simply collapsed in their hallway, reaching for his coat. I have no idea what they ate and drank that night. He was nine years younger than I. Seemingly healthy and full of nervous energy. We'd lived together for just short of three years. He thought that was good enough for me, and what was I going to do? There was something murky going on underneath. I wasn't going to give any ultimatum. He didn't want to get married. Not to me anyway. And that was that. Was it that I was already too old to give him a whole bunch of children? That's what I told myself on good days. On bad days, I told myself I simply wasn't good enough in his eyes. He never introduced me to his family, not in all our time living together. It's true, I made my living as a secretary, never went to college, and he was an attorney. But I paid my share of our living expenses, and my share turned out to be larger than what I had paid when I lived by myself in an efficiency apartment before moving in with him. At times I thought I merely stayed because my ego insisted I was owed something. His arrogance was enormous. I suspect I met his needs well enough. His greatest need was to be better than someone. In his eyes, I fit that bill. So much so that I gradually came to believe it myself.

His family's arrogance was even larger. When he unexpectedly died, they curtly informed me I wasn't welcome at his memorial or his funeral, though I had been welcome in his bed. The ceremonies were reserved for family and friends, not lovers. I didn't count. I wasn't his widow. If I had been important enough to him, he would have married me. He didn't, and so, for all practical purposes, I didn't exist. Jeff didn't leave a will either. So, when he died, I simply moved out of the apartment, letting his family scramble about the lease and all his belongings. I didn't have much. Found an efficiency apartment again. Rents had gone up in those three years. I could just manage it though. I visited his grave once to say goodbye. He wasn't a bad guy. He wasn't a particularly good one either.

Sometimes I felt maybe I was not meant for love, neither loving nor being loved. I wanted to give all of myself. And then there were all these diminishments. Jeff wasn't proud to be with me. If anything, he was ashamed of me, my lack of education, my lack of pedigree, that sort of thing. Not that he was anything special in the pedigree department, but I guess being a lawyer was way up there in the of-consequence milieu. I think if I lived in a society where higher education wasn't so expensive, I could have been his equal. But the way our world was set up, he had enough clout and nerve to sign up for student loans. I didn't. Maybe it's good we weren't married. I might have ended up being responsible for his student loan balance. I have no idea, and since I was so unwelcome by his snooty family, I didn't take the time and trouble to find out.

I was prepared to wander the back alleys of life once again, just so as not to be a burden on anyone. Cockroaches. Drunks hollering or retching into garbage bins in the middle of the night outside my window. At least in that milieu nobody was looking down on me. Now I don't quite know how to handle the open door to a better life. Martin says I'm free to do whatever I like. We can afford it. I could stay at home. Quit my job. Even go to college at long last and get a degree in something. I don't know. I should be ecstatic. I'm married to a generous man. I stand here on the balcony in fairytale surroundings. The air is getting warmer now, though there are still goosebumps on my arms. I'm afraid of feeling like an outsider for the rest of my life.

Three small people walk on the sand down below close to one another. Picking up shells? Trash? Lost valuables?

And here is Martin's voice now from inside our luxurious suite.

"Are you ready to go down for breakfast?"

I don't know if I am ready for anything.

"Yes," I say and turn to go inside.

Mardi Gras

She drove through hard rain. She never made it to downtown New Orleans. Instead, she bought red and gold beads at a suburban chain store. It was the extent of her remaining energy that day. Mardi Gras downtown would have given her bragging rights.

The rain kept pouring down in sheets. She needed to get to the ocean, for comfort, for a roar of yesterday.

She knew it was the last time she had seen her first love. His gentle wife interpreted his final mumble: *See ya*, he said. A lift of his hand, fingers splayed.

She remembered their first kiss at seventeen. The ground had shifted. Later, living on a budget, they shared hope, cockroaches, spaghetti, intellectual pursuits, double-feature discount movies, and once, in a small theater in Paris, a play where Camus' Caligula sprayed them with spittle, so close were they to the action on stage.

He was brilliant and athletic, and he wouldn't dance. Still, he was her hero. In time she grew impatient with his inadvertent masculine disdain. She loved, she adored, she shrank, she got confused. One day she left one last, irrevocable time. She wondered how she could have convinced him to see her. One time he had called her exquisite.

At night, approaching Galveston, the rain had almost stopped. Remembering him cling to life made her ache to be a better person. That wish would likely dissolve in future distractions.

She found a parking lot overlooking the sea and folded back her seat. She fell asleep worrying, what if anybody asked her: *Why did you ever leave him?* How could she possibly explain? It was too dark to see the water, she just knew it was there.

She needn't have worried so much. Nobody ever asked.

Young, Old, Between

Hers

Blues and greens glint in the windows of The Mermaid Parlor. Tiny sequins, I think. I always like to see behind the magic of things.

The four of us sit on a lacquered bench outside, Gordon in deep conversation about Snow White with nine-year-old Elena. I am proud of him for being so conversant in fairy tales with our two daughters. You wouldn't expect it of him, a Vietnam vet with horrors lurking in his soul that I know exceed anything in the grimmest of Grimm's Fairy Tales. I love the sweetness and seriousness with which he honors our daughters and their preoccupations. In the warm breeze, I indulge in my own daydreams, so I am not following their conversation. He must have just said something hilarious because Elena bursts into a peal of laughter before she resumes licking daintily around the outside of the pale green ice cream in her waffle cone.

Cindy, only seven and a half, sits next to me petting the plush pink rabbit in her lap. She won it three days ago in a shop on the boardwalk just half a block down from where we are sitting now, and she hasn't parted from it for even a minute except to take a bath, and even then, it lies on the closed toilet lid right next to the tub. When she goes into the ocean, and she never goes far, she keeps it high against her shoulder and it has never yet fallen in. She, too, is now studying Gordon and Elena while stroking the rabbit's pink fur. Suddenly I see slow tears rolling down her cheeks.

"Cindy, what's the matter?" I touch her wet cheek.

"She has an ice cream," Cindy says.

I don't think this is the time to point out that when we were at the ice cream stand a few minutes earlier, she didn't want one. "Come on, I'll get you one," I say instead.

Cindy avoids my eyes and turns her head from side to side as tears keep rolling. "I want hers."

Elena has heard this and already holds out her still amply filled waffle cone. "Here."

"No," Cindy whispers. She keeps shaking her head slowly and looking down into her lap at the pink rabbit that now catches a few of her tears.

I understand exactly what she means. The joy. The laughter. And at this moment none of us know how to give it to her.

Cornflowers

Cornflowers were his favorites. I didn't know my grandfather well. We lived a twelve-hour train ride apart. I remember him slender, quite handsome, soft-spoken, and very kind.

Cornflowers were one of my mother's favorites too. She had told me many times about walking hand in hand with her father after her own mother had died, through wheat fields and rye fields he owned before the war, learning the names of flowers and birds, and learning to trust the comfort of his familiar presence.

When he died suddenly many years later, she was inconsolable. She had taken it for granted he would always be there. There was no one she could leave me with, my father being out of town on business, so she took me along on her journey of saying goodbye.

I remember her tears, the wrenching sound of her sobs. I remember the soot on the windows in the train, the greasy spots on the heavy brown curtains, the dusty smell of unplanned travel.

Her stepmother, only a few years older than my own mother, greeted us with shaky smiles and one of the few hugs that Germans would take the liberty of exchanging in that era of stoic handshakes.

On the day of the funeral there were wreaths of lilies and white roses and fragrant green fir and spruce. My mother looked haunted, pale, and beautiful in her black dress.

With wreaths and seven siblings and extended families and a shortage of cars, some of us walked to the funeral. It wasn't far.

We walked past fields. It was June. Cornflowers were in bloom. I had recently learned how to braid flowers into a wreath. So I plucked flowers from the edge of the fields as we walked and started braiding them to send along with him. Some of them were hard to pluck and scored the skin of my fingers. Still, it was the one useful thing I could think of doing, being small and typically superfluous in the company of adults.

One of my aunts decided to upbraid me: "What a vain child. Here we are going to her grandfather's funeral, and she is making a wreath for her hair."

"No, it's a wreath for his grave," I explained.

She looked as though she didn't believe me or else preferred to stick with her own interpretation. My beautiful sad mother was too busy grieving to come to my aid, and so I had a first lesson in needing to steel myself against a life of much misinterpretation.

The Gift

A jig of laughter pulsed in Kaly's head: 'I want, I want.' Sometimes she wanted honey. Other times colors. Or crystals, dresses, and little girl jewelry. Ice cream. A red plush teddy bear.

"No," she yelled when Todd took all the rolls and lined them up on his plate. "There's enough for everybody."

"Oh, no, there isn't." He grinned, then touched her nose. "Don't look so tragic, little sister. I'm only trying to teach you stuff."

"What?"

"That you have to guard your breakfast rolls instead of daydreaming. This isn't paradise, you know."

"What's paradise?"

"I'll tell you later." He put one roll on her plate and two back in the basket before he pushed his chair back.

"No, tell me now." She covered her roll with her hands.

"Ever heard of entropy?"

"No."

"Well, it's like some sort of magic. Everything that touches something else becomes a little less."

"So, one day there really won't be enough?"

"Bingo. That's what you learn in school. Jeez, I got to fly. I'll be late."

She wanted to go, too, but she was little and too delicate.

The front door closed with a bang. Mommy's shoulders twitched. But then she looked as though she hadn't even noticed. It was only Todd anyway.

Good thing Daddy had left earlier, otherwise he might get mad at Todd again. Which he did more often than not. Kaly thought trying to be perfect was their best bet, but Todd disagreed. He said being perfect was useless. Daddy would be mad no matter what. Maybe Todd was right.

Kaly blew at hot chocolate steam coming out of her mug. You could get just so close and no closer, otherwise it stung your nose. The steam swirled. She tried to blow it around the little bluebell elf on the mug handle, to tell her that she was thinking about her and trying to keep her warm. Todd had told her that that's how you made mist in movies, with lots of steam. But she couldn't get the steam to go down, except a little, not far enough. And then it didn't stay down. The blue elf's name was Melina, and she'd just have to do without mist.

Kaly nibbled on her roll and followed the honey with her tongue, down the left side of her mouth, until she caught most of it. When Mommy wasn't watching, Kaly placed her tongue on Melina's face to share the honey taste. Then she held her roll at an angle to make all the honey still in it flow back into the center.

Mommy got up and turned on the blue plastic radio. They were alone now. It was a good time of day. Everyone else gone. Daddy to work, Todd to school. The two of them would just sit here.

Mommy turned on the computer at the desk by the window and sat down to start her morning ritual of putting sheets of paper from a shrinking stack on the left side to a growing stack on her right.

That was a Canadian chanteuse on the radio. Kaly paid special attention to it because this chanteuse was Mommy's favorite singer. Kaly could recognize her voice anywhere now. Chanteuse was the first, and so far only, French word that Kaly knew. It meant singer. This one sang a lot of love songs, both loud and whispery.

When Mommy was done typing and printing, she came back to the table to compare the papers, the new ones from the printer to the old ones. She made her index fingers move down two sheets at the same time, then flipped them over and started on top of the next sheet. It looked graceful.

Kaly couldn't help because she didn't know how to read or write yet. She wanted to know desperately, but she was sick too often. That and being young was a lousy combination. It was the reason for not being allowed to go to pre-school.

Mommy was beautiful. Kaly liked her best in a cornflower blue dress, but she didn't wear it often. Usually, she just put on a pair of jeans with any old top. Today's top had thin spots at the shoulder seams and under the arms, which was a surprise, because the document man would come today.

"Do you like dresses, Mommy?"

"On you I do."

"No, on yourself, I mean," Kaly said.

"Oh, yeah. Sometimes."

Kaly herself was lucky. She got to wear a dark red velvet tunic over her tights, like a dress, and the reason she had something so beautiful was because it was a hand-me-down from her cousin. Now it belonged to Kaly. Velvet was good because princesses wore it.

Kaly finished nearly all of her roll and licked every bit of the honey she could get to out of its center. She slid from her chair to her feet with a small thump.

Mommy looked up. "Did you finish your breakfast?"

"Yes. Except maybe one bite," Kaly said.

"That's okay then," Mommy said.

"I'll clear the table," Kaly said.

"You think you can?"

"Sure, I can." Kaly squared her shoulders and took plates and mugs and silverware, one by one, from the table to the serving counter that divided the kitchen and dining room areas. She left only her mug on the table. It still had hot chocolate in it. Someday she would be someone important in a velvet dress of all kinds of colors. Maybe even embroidered with seed pearls. She loved seed pearls. They made her think of flowers they might one day become. Then she would buy a castle for Mommy. Or maybe even just a big, wonderful house. She now went around to the other side of the serving counter and took the dishes from there to the sink.

"Thanks, Kaly." Mommy's voice sounded like the

honey Kaly had just eaten, golden.

What Kaly wanted most of all now was a set of color crayons, like the one she got from Todd for her last birthday, but better. The set from Todd had twelve crayons. The one she wanted now was bigger. Like, huge. She didn't even know how many were in there, but she'd seen one. There were all kinds of colors in there. Pistachio green, for example. For meadows and the edge of lakes. Yes. Also purple, for flowers and skies. Ice blue for a day like this.

At nine o'clock the doorbell rang.

It was the document man. He came once or twice a week to pick up typed documents and bring new ones to do.

"Good morning, Mr. Lyons."

He brought in the scent of snow on his clothes. But he wore leather gloves and didn't have to blow on his hands. He wasn't in a good mood today. When Mommy brought him into the room, he smiled at Kaly. But his lips were compressed, the way Daddy's lips looked before he stood up to slap Todd.

Mommy knew too that the document man wasn't in a good mood. She held her head low and made her shoulders small.

Usually, Mr. Lyons was in and out of their place, but today he carefully pulled off his gloves and let Mommy bring him a cup of coffee. Which he banged on the table, splattering some on the white tablecloth. That was probably okay since it was only plastic.

"Oh, sorry." In his voice he wasn't sorry at all. Mommy said it didn't matter.

He started looking at the finished papers that Mommy had in five different folders. He opened one folder, another, flipped through the pages to inspect them. He kept nodding. A few times, though, he stopped to hold out a sheet.

"Please," he said. "Be really meticulous with all of these. This one will do, but if the print doesn't come out well, you'll have to change the cartridge."

Kaly wondered what 'meticulous' meant.

"Sorry," Mommy said, and she did mean it. Because

cartridges were expensive.

He went through each folder and found a few more pages he didn't like.

"I have good news and bad news for you," he said. "I can bring you lots more work from now on. But I can't pay you as much as I paid before. Everybody's trying to economize, and nobody wants to pay a lot anymore. And they always find folks to do it for less."

"How much?" Mommy asked.

"Well." He rasped in this throat, then recited some numbers. Kaly couldn't follow what he said. She wasn't good at numbers, even simple ones. She didn't like his voice.

"But I'll be working hours and hours more and still be making the same," Mommy said.

"Well, look at it this way. At least you will be making the same and not less," he said.

After he left, Mommy sat down at the table and pushed the folders he had brought out of reach. Then she put her head on the tabletop with her arms circled around it and cried.

"Mommy." Kaly came to her mother's side and touched the fine brown curls spreading on the table. They were soft and trembled under Kaly's hand.

"I'm tired," Mommy said. "I'll be okay."

"Like when I feel sick?" Kaly asked.

"Yeah."

"Maybe you should go to bed, then," Kaly said. Mommy did look tired, at ten o'clock in the morning, and her face felt hot.

"I'll be fine, Kaly. Go play for a bit." Kaly didn't know whether that meant Mommy really wanted her to go away, or did she maybe want her to stay after all. Kaly hovered and let her hand rest on Mommy's hair. Now she could feel it more clearly. Go play this time meant go away, leave me alone. So, she went away. But not far.

She didn't feel like playing. It was cold. She tiptoed to the bookshelf by the window, pulled a chair to it and climbed up to look at the photographs. In case her mother needed something later, she'd still be in the room.

She loved the picture of Mommy and Daddy when they got married. They only had Todd then. Odd to imagine a world in which she didn't exist. Mommy looked happy and wore a lacy dress. Daddy looked nicer on the photograph than how she knew him. Maybe he had been nicer then. She couldn't remember ever having seen him so friendly and happy. Was it something to do with her? She'd have to ask Todd sometime if Daddy had been friendlier when she wasn't around. Todd would know, because he had been small then and would have had time to notice, just as she always noticed things.

Mommy looked like a true princess of the sun in the photo. She should always be beautiful like that.

Kaly wished she could give Mommy a gift. Kaly always felt wonderful when she was sick and someone gave her a gift. But she had nothing to give. Especially not that important stuff everybody was always talking about. Money. For which you could get everything else. Some time ago, she had thirty-five cents. But then she bought Mommy a candy bar for her birthday, and now she had none. There was nothing she could do to help.

Suddenly, though, she knew what she could give.

It felt like fireworks inside of her. Lots of color. Lots of sparks. All the stuff other kids had burned up in those sparks. All the interesting store displays she had ever seen. The books. The beautiful papers. The ribbons. The crayons. Especially the crayons. They all sparked up in jubilation as Kaly's life changed forever.

She would never want or ask for anything again. Especially not from Mommy. That would be her gift. Not wanting anything. Not needing anything. She saw a tiny bubble of water on the glass that covered the photographs, but when she wiped at it, it turned out that it wasn't there at all. Her heart felt very large and golden, like a stone reaching up to learn how to fly.

She thought of Abraham and Isaac, hoping that something would appear and make it unnecessary after all.

But nothing appeared.

She turned around to look at Mommy, who still had her head in the circle of her arms. Kaly walked back to the table and touched Mommy's arm lightly. She didn't say a word but thought with huge intention how everything would be alright now.

Melina on her hot chocolate mug handle looked dumb and snippety, a little like a gargoyle. But that was Melina's problem. Kaly had more important things to worry about now.

The Dollhouse

It was listed in the newspaper in late October. Each week in November you had to go to a different one of the four stores that sponsored the contest and get a dated voucher. When you had collected all four, you would submit them at the newspaper main office together with your age. You had to be under twelve to qualify. Then in December a drawing would be held, and on December 18, in time for Christmas, the winner would receive the most magnificent dollhouse Nina had ever seen. It was on display in a window by the newspaper's main entrance. It was two full stories high, with an additional low steepled tower in which a tiny white cat lay curled up. Stairs in the center led from one floor to the next. The first floor had two rooms, the second floor had three, all filled with exquisite old-fashioned wood-carved furniture, tiny carpets, mirrors, and draperies. No kitchen or bathroom, but dollhouses rarely had those. Nina fell in love at first sight, especially with the white cat in the attic space, because they couldn't have a real cat at home. They had tried once and had to return the cat because it had climbed her mother's lace curtains, and that was unacceptable. Nina just knew the dollhouse was meant to be hers.

Mrs. Willow knew needing to visit the stores to get the vouchers was almost as effective a marketing strategy as the slide next to the conventional stairway that led down to the basement children's department in the shoe store on Carolina Street, with one essential difference: a growing child's shoes had to be replaced, no option for hand-me-downs there, and the opportunity for a child to slide down to a necessary purchase was priceless. In contrast, the stores that sponsored the dollhouse sold things rather less essential: jewelry, fine furniture, fabric, and liquor. She was prepared to face and resist the sales tactics in all four stores for her daughter's sake. She was more worried about the potential, and to her mind very likely, disappointment her daughter might be about to experience.

Nina's older brother Peter, due to a visitor occupying his room, temporarily shared his little sister's room. He heard Nina's nightly prayers in early November, and he decided to take things into his own hands in case God should fail to come through for his beloved sister. At first, he kept it a secret even from their parents, but after a while his limited funds as well as his expertise dried up and he needed their assistance. He used particle board as a base, then sawed, carved, glued, and painted balsa wood for walls, and, with Mrs. Willow's help, selected furnishings and a miniature doll, to be purchased on the 19th of December, should they be required.

On the 18th of December, Nina was disconsolate. The photo in the newspaper showed a curly-headed girl with two missing front teeth grinning next to her prize, the dollhouse that should have been Nina's. The prize had been given a day early so that the photo could appear in the paper on the day of the official award.

"I prayed and prayed," Nina told her mother between sobs. "It was supposed to be mine. I was sure."

"I imagine the other girl prayed too, and God had to make a choice," Mrs. Willow tried to explain.

"You don't understand. He should have chosen me. I loved it. I wanted it so much."

Mr. Willow for his part offered an entire chocolate bar with hazelnuts, not just a single piece, and Nina accepted it grudgingly. It did not help her get over her bitterness.

On Christmas Eve, she found and cheerfully played with a two-room dollhouse suite she found under the Christmas tree. It had sparse contemporary furniture, including a few pictures on the walls made from postage stamps. It also had a three-tree garden complete with a patio and green sandpaper lawn and a small pond made of blue paint and smoothed to a watery shine with transparent glue. There was a tiny deck chair on the patio, and a black poodle fashioned from flexible pipe cleaners lay by the chair, since Peter had no idea about Nina's love for a curled up white cat in a tower. Three little geese stood by the pond.

Peter had hoped Nina would say, "Oh, just what I wanted." She was, however, so young that for the longest time she didn't even register a connection between her prayers and the ranch style dollhouse, even as she played with it on Christmas Eve and in the weeks to come. Peter didn't want to say anything, partly because he was disappointed that his gift had not exactly come up to snuff, and partly because he was afraid that he had unduly interfered with God's plans for Nina by trying to help out God who was then free to assume the dollhouse was taken care of and who could now direct His attention elsewhere.

Mr. and Mrs. Willow didn't know what to say either. They wanted to explain to Nina the value of the love that had come her way, but they didn't have the right words, so they let it be.

Not until years after the event and many other discrepancies between expectations and reality did Nina realize the ways in which her prayers had after all been answered with gentleness, enthusiasm, and love to which she had been oblivious. And so the stage was set for a lifetime of blessings, some of which were instead perceived as disappointments. Indeed, sometimes she got what she wanted and barely even noticed. She stopped praying and decided it would be best to not set her hopes too high and to muddle through circumstances as best she could. Still, until the end of her days she yearned for a God who would see the world exactly the way she did.

Summer Music

Monday, June 20

Dear Diary,

Well, at least I have the comfort here of writing this like a real letter, on paper, old-fashioned as that might be, in this gorgeous leatherbound notebook Arlan gave me for my birthday. It feels special. Not like "Hi, Diary" or "Yo, iPad." It's so beautiful, and it smells good, almost too beautiful to use up for everyday stuff, but I'll do it anyway. Treat myself with beauty. Spoil myself a little.

The best thing ever happened today. Miss Terry emailed and asked me to turn the pages for her at her organ concerts next Friday and Sunday, both. Of course, I emailed back YES in capital letters. I've done it for her before on Sunday during the service, but this is different. Two whole forty-five-minute concerts. She'll know the music by heart anyway, so it's all just in case. Still, it's a safety net she wants, and I'm thrilled she asked me. She always gives this very stern nod when she wants the page turned. It looks impatient, almost angry, but it isn't. She's just focused and intense.

I wish I were more talented.

I love playing with her name. Miss Terry. Mystery. And I'm probably not the only one, but nobody has ever said anything out loud. That I know of. Teresa Summer. I'm glad she lets us call her by her first name, even with the Miss added to it.

Tuesday, June 21

Dear Diary—this is the last time I'll call you that. After today, I'll just start writing.

In music appreciation in camp today, Mr. Wheat told us about Vivaldi's time as musician in residence at the Ospedale della Pietà. That was an orphanage in Venice and the orphan girls there were all taught music. What a wonderful concept. But what made the biggest impression on me was the thing that, once taught and of a certain age, they were paraded in the streets of Venice (I thought Venice only had canals!—just kidding), so that the men of the city could have their pick of them. I imagine them with their lutes and flutes and drums, probably in white dresses, wandering along and hoping to be picked. Or hoping not to be picked as the case might be. It sort of reminds me of dances in the gym where you're hanging around waiting for some guy to ask you to dance, or else just dancing with your girlfriends, pretending you're not paying attention to the guys at all. And, sure, you can ask a guy, but then you run the risk of being ridiculed as forward, fast, in short, slutty. Meanwhile if you do the right thing and wait till someone asks you, chances are it's not someone you want. It's complicated.

When I got home, I went on the internet to see if I could find out more about when and where and how those parades took place, but I couldn't find much. That they were taught music, yes, and even something about how some of the more talented girls were picked out by some members of the nobility and how two girls, or women, females in any event, lived with Vivaldi, but platonically. But nothing about those parades. Did Mr. Wheat make that up? Doesn't seem like him, but who knows. Anyway, I'll probably do more research, maybe do an essay on it. I sure can't get those girls out of my mind. Did they get a chance to say no and stay in the Ospedale? Or did they have to go if someone picked them for the great honor of having the chance to cook his dinners, sew his shirts, and pluck his chickens? Mr. Wheat said sometimes such a marriage was contracted within an hour. I couldn't find anything about that either. Were they afraid of being picked? Afraid of not being picked? I imagine one of them lying in bed at night. Mother Mary, please let nobody pick me. Unless is were Giuseppe, the painter who sometimes comes to refresh the walls in the chapel. I imagine one girl crying because she has to go with the wart-nosed butcher. I imagine another one crying because nobody wanted her at all.

Do I dare ask Mr. Wheat if he can tell me where I can learn more, not about his beloved Vivaldi, but about those girls?

Wednesday, June 22

We had choir practice last night. It's so different from Miss Terry's children's choir. Where I was just recently the tallest, the oldest, and the one most likely to get a solo part. Now I'm just one of a whole bunch of all sorts of people. About fifteen minutes into choir practice, Pastor Weber breezed in to lead the practice, and Miss Terry, as always, graciously let him take over the reins. Even though she's the professional musician and he is just a hobby musician, though two of his sons are studying music at university, so music is clearly in the family.

I prefer it when she leads the choir practice. I think Mom does too. It feels less stressful somehow.

Dad picked Mom and me up from choir practice so we wouldn't have to walk. It's not far, but it's in the old part of town and it's late at night by the time we're done. When Miss Terry came out the door of the parish hall with us, Dad tried one of his wanna-be charming old guy flirtations with her. I didn't hear what he said to her, but I could tell she wasn't pleased, and she said something in response that didn't float his boat either, because when we were in the car, he grumbled.

"That old spinster. She needs to lighten up. What she needs is a man."

I wanted to defend her and point out that she isn't old at all, but when Dad is in that kind of mood, it's best to stay mum. Mom didn't say anything either. It bugged me, though, what he said about her needing a man. Someone like him?

Thursday, June 23

Well, my lesson with Miss Terry sure was fascinating today. I hadn't practiced all week except maybe a half an hour or forty-five minutes last Friday. There's always so much going on and on top of that I'm supposed to find an hour a day to practice the piano. Every day! So, I felt a bit guilty when I sat next to her on her piano bench. The piece I am supposed to be practicing is the Bach praeludium that I actually like a whole lot. It's one of Mom's favorites too, so, go figure. I just didn't have time to practice. There is life too, you know? Not just music.

Anyway, so I sat next to her, steeling myself against an anticipated reprimand, though come to think of it, she's never been like that. Never scolds, never gets mad, never makes me feel incompetent. She's actually a very good teacher. But whenever I deal with adults, there's always the shadowy anticipation of being in trouble for doing something wrong. So, I mustered all my energy to play what I was, by my own judgment, ill prepared for playing. I gave it all I had—given that I had nothing. When I stopped, I sat there silently expecting a relatively kind admonishment to practice more. Instead, she looked at me with moist eyes.

"That was incredible," she said. "Best I've ever heard you play."

Oh, boy! Relief. And impostor guilt as well. Fooled you, didn't I? I was absolutely baffled, of course. Still am. What does it mean? That the point of life is fooling other people? That it doesn't really matter what I do? That it's all a fluke? I was pleased too at the moment of receiving praise where I really didn't deserve it, not like that anyway. Something in this life is always wrong. And incomprehensible. For next week, I'm supposed to add a Beethoven sonatina. We'll see how that goes. It's a lively one, not too many chords. I'm better at nimble fingering than at playing chords. My hands seem to be too small to play too many notes all at once.

Another thing she told me during the lesson was that I looked like Brigitte Bardot. I had no clue who that was, so she told me, an old movie star who was famous last century. So, I looked her up online and I don't look anything like her at all. Maybe the blond hair, but that's it.

I do wish I had more talent. I'm never going to be a great pianist. I take these lessons because Mom thinks I should. But for what, when all is said and done? No prince or duke is going to come along and prefer me to all other girls or women just because I know how to play the piano a little. If I had talent, presumably I could become a musician like Miss Terry. She is fantastic. She really, really loves music. And yet, when all is said and done, nobody outside our congregation has ever heard of her. She gives two or three organ concerts a year, plays every Sunday for two church services, one at 8 o'clock and another at 10 o'clock, and leads our choir. And that's it. I hope she is happy. Perhaps she is. Today she wore a red blouse which looked quite nice on her. I don't think I've ever seen her wear anything besides black in the past. And it's not mourning or anything like that. I think she wears black because it suits her, makes her look stunning, and she doesn't have to make a choice of what to wear each and every day. Except today. I think maybe I'll wear all black too for a while. It feels so interesting. Though I know the French woman at the perfume shop who wears only white. Her reason: when she grew up, there were constant funerals and mourning periods that once she was an adult, she vowed to always wear white and above all never black again.

Friday, June 24

Tonight is the night. The first concert. I only get to turn the pages, but it still feels as though it's somehow mine. I wonder how I would have done back in Venice in Vivaldi's days. Would I have been chosen to play an instrument, and if so, which one? Maybe I'd be in the choir. I still don't think I would like to be paraded in the street for the prospect of being picked as someone's wife. I can imagine being busy with children and cooking and keeping the chickens and whatever else we owned, maybe a sheep or a goat. I think if I were in Vivaldi's Venice, I'd rather stay in a convent and make music. Or take care of the chickens there.

I am so excited about tonight.

Saturday, June 25

The concert was fantastic. She really nailed it. She is so beautiful, too. Short black curls, and the tiniest bit of a shadow of a moustache on her upper lip. Like a mysterious gypsy woman.

I got there half an hour early of course, like I was supposed to. And I looked down from the balcony and saw that half the church was already filled with people. I told her to come look, but she said no. She preferred not to know whether there were five people or fifty or five hundred. "That way it's between me and God. And the music," she said. People just make her nervous. God and music don't.

Then, just before she started playing, she told me that sometimes in the middle of the night when she feels particularly sad or happy, she comes and plays just by herself. The church is too far from any of the nearby buildings for anyone to hear, so it doesn't matter what time of night it is. Then she can play whatever she wants, and she doesn't need anybody on standby to turn her pages. She has the key to the side door of the church of course. I wonder if it feels spooky in the staircase up to the balcony in the middle of the night, with the church gaping dark and empty below her. And probably daddy-long-legs in the corners. I've never seen one on the organ bench, or inside it, for that matter, where she keeps stacks of sheet music. It would be such a good place to hide for a creepy critter. Even a church mouse.

Sunday, June 26

I do wish I had more talent. If music loved me back, it wouldn't be so hard to practice an hour a day or even more. I want to cry, and I really don't have a reason to.

Last night, I dreamt of a young woman. She didn't say a word, but she thought words to me. *When the girls sing, it hurts. It brings back memories.* But then there was a snarling white dog that woke me up from inside my dream. Thank God it was only a dream.

I like to think of Miss Terry up on the balcony all by herself in the middle of the night playing her music no matter what, knowing that it is enough to lure the most dreamy magic from the manual keys and the wooden pedal board. Tonight, I get to turn the pages for her again. As for me, I am yearning for a place I can go to in the middle of the night to be myself.

Two Roman Soldiers

Her English teacher called her Mousy, perhaps because she often wore a wooden mouse pin with red rhinestone eyes and a thin leather strip for a tail. She didn't mind. The pin had been her mother's idea of adorable. There was a lot of confusion in those days. Roman soldiers didn't particularly float her boat, for instance. All the same, she wrote a story about two of them once, and to her enormous surprise, her teacher, a former Jesuit priest, now happily married to a former nun and teaching at her Lutheran all-girls school, was so impressed with her story, he asked if he could have it. She was flattered and said of course and handed over her exercise book, almost empty otherwise. Since she wasn't interested in Roman soldiers in the first place and soon couldn't remember what she had written, she was hardly going to miss the story. Not long afterwards, the school decided to let the teacher go. Some of his views were considered too radical for an all-girls school. This in contrast to one of the Latin teachers who was rumored to have an affair with either another teacher or one of the older students; he got away with a stern warning.

Meanwhile what did fiercely interest her were boys and her feelings about one or the other. There was, for example, a gorgeous blond boy who on warm late summer afternoons sat at a street corner opposite the public library and played his guitar, surrounded by friends and whoever else wanted to listen. Sometimes he sang. His long blond hair fell into his face as he bent over his guitar, and she was lost. She liked the sight of him almost more than the music, though he played songs she knew and liked. She couldn't possibly go up to him and tell him how beautiful he was and how much she would like to kiss him. It just wasn't done. One day, though, she talked to one of his friends in the periphery of the circle around him, and, to her surprise, got not only the boy's name but also his phone number, which she carried around for two weeks before calling him from a yellow public payphone booth. He wasn't at home, however, and she only got to talk to his father for a few minutes. His father was friendly but somewhat condescending and not very helpful, didn't suggest a call back time or ask for a call back number. She never tried calling again. She walked by the corner opposite the library many more times just in case. After all, there were always books to borrow and return. But it was chillier now, and it rained often, and nobody was ever there again. Perhaps she had scared the beautiful guitar player away? It was difficult to tell.

When it didn't rain, she now took solitary walks around City Lake, heard frogs a few times, looked at the last of the hardy flowers that remained, and shuffled through the fallen leaves on the ground. When it did rain, she stayed home and wrote about the boy. She didn't give his name and didn't make one up for him either. She simply called him the blond boy and wrote how his image drew her to the lake, luring her with laughter and a few songs, and so she followed. Around and around they went, swaying and gliding to some magical music no one else could hear. How she longed for him in those musings. The rest of the world could only hear the traffic of the city, now and again a siren, the yapping of dogs, bird calls, and squirrels rustling in the fallen leaves, and once in a while a shrill whistle, probably summoning some dog.

By now she had a new English teacher, and when she showed him the story which still made her skin prickle when she read it to herself, he looked into her eyes briefly, then looked away. "I don't know what to say," he said. She thanked him and took her exercise book back, preparing to wonder for the rest of her days if it would have been better had she once more written about two Roman soldiers. Even had she wanted to, though, she couldn't remember a word of what she had written about them before. After all, they hadn't interested her in the least.

Summer Days

At first there were only a few Canada geese, five or six, then ten, eleven, twelve, all busy with sparse summer grass. Twelve were about all that fit on the tiny triangle of land that formed the tip of the lower part of the island. Willow loved the long curves of their necks and the efficient clip of their beaks. She had seen the island on her walk home from shopping in the downtown pedestrian shopping zone and come with her sketchbook. Geese were always a good subject for sketching. There was even a willow on the banks of the river opposite where she chose to sit. That in itself had to be a good sign.

Until fifth grade, she had thought her given name was special. So had her parents. Plus, her mother's brother, who had died in a car crash before she was born, had been called William. But in September of fifth grade, there had been not two, not three, but four Willows in her class, including her. The following year, the other three Willows were gone again. Families were always moving in and out of town these days, though hers had lived here all her life and there was no plan to ever move. Her best friend, Lisha, too, had been here for all that time, and her family, too, had no intention of moving away. Lisha was a nickname derived from Letitia, and unfortunately she was no great use during the summer, only during the school year. Lisha was strait-laced and never went anywhere for exploratory jaunts, not even shopping, unless it was with her family, which was then awkward for Willow, always provided she was asked along in the first place. Lisha didn't go dancing or to parties, she hadn't even participated in the school-sponsored dancing lessons. She wasn't a member of the youth choir. Nothing. The only extracurricular event Lisha ever attended was a monthly series of concerts and plays during the school year. So, for summer vacation, Willow was pretty much on her own. She was a bit tired of the bland flavor of boredom in her days.

Being bored felt undignified, though. She tried her best to at least not look undignified. Everybody else always seemed to be so full of energy and adventure. Most of the other kids she knew were away on trips somewhere. She yearned for some adventure of her own.

Willow had been coming every day for a week when a group of five young people, older than her, maybe in their twenties, came down the seven steps from the upper level of the island with its street vendors. They were laughing and having a boisterously good time. Four guys and one woman. Two of the guys had guitar cases on their backs. That drew Willow's interest. That and their hair, long hair on the men. In fact, the woman's hair was the shortest of the lot, in a pixie cut, bleached blond with uneven purple ends.

To make room for the newcomers, Willow moved as close to the tip of the little island as was possible without danger of falling in. The geese had all left with a great big swoosh at the boisterous descent of the five young people. In order to look busy, Willow pretended to study her current drawing in her sketch book, this one of the stone wall edging the island, parts of it polished slick by the water, the rest covered with patches of moss.

"Let me see," one of the guys said behind her.

"I haven't figured out yet how to draw the soft look of the moss," Willow said.

"Looks pretty good to me," the guy said. The woman gave Willow a wary glance. *Come on*, Willow wanted to say. *I'm just a high school student. No competition for you.* But she held her tongue.

From then on, some of them came to the island every day. Usually, it was just the four guys. She learned their names. Angelo, Mark, Jeddy, and Fred. The name Angelo made her giggle. What kind of name was that for a guy? He decidedly did not look like an angel. Stubble on his cheeks, and a tooth halfway to the left of his mouth was missing, not right out front but still visible. He was friendly enough, though, almost shy. The woman's name was Dora, but she rarely came. The guys told Willow they slept under one of the bridges in bivy sacks. Truly. Though obviously not in the commercial center of town. Sometimes in graveyards, one of them added. Willow didn't know whether to believe them. There were no bivy sacks or sleeping bags in evidence, just the two guitars which belonged to Angelo and Jeddy. They did play from time to time, and they sounded pretty good, especially Angelo. They reminded Willow of the time she had gone to a rock concert by a high school band, and she'd gone backstage to talk to the guitarist who had looked attractive. She was gushing compliments, and he thanked her but acted unsure as to what to do about her and her backstage appearance. It had certainly not led to any kind of groupie encounter of the sort she read about in her teen magazines.

Angelo and Jeddy, probably due to their age, acted more experienced. Willow wasn't physically attracted to them or the other guys, which was just as well because they felt out of her league, age-wise and in other respects as well. They seemed sophisticated in ways she found intriguing. They were certainly not the kind of guys to take home and introduce to her parents. She knew her parents wouldn't approve of them. They clearly didn't live anywhere in town permanently, though they had to manage to get a shower or a bath from time to time. They didn't smell homeless. They didn't appear to have jobs either and they seemed to be too old to be students, though one could presumably be a student at any age. She didn't want to ask at first because she didn't want to come across as nosy, and later it always felt wrong to ask, as though she should have known all along. One day she might find out. Not that it mattered.

On the much larger upper level of the island, a small boutique with beautiful clothes often brought some of the merchandise outside on racks. There was a blue and green long dress Willow thought was beautiful. She didn't have enough money at the moment. Besides, hanging out with these guys down below required jeans and inconspicuous T-shirts, not flowing gowns. She sometimes considered the idea of flirting with one of these guys, but she couldn't decide on which one. Angelo maybe. When he played his guitar and bent over it, looking down on the strings, his long hair fell into his face which made him look absorbed and mysterious. She liked that. Normally he looked pretty ordinary apart from the missing tooth. At times she had imaginary conversations with her parents or other authority figures, defending the guys' long hair. Jesus, after all, consistently had long hair, and nobody had any objections to that, did they? But these conversations never came up in reality, which was just as well.

Willow was surprised when she saw the first leaves tumble down from a tree across the water in a gust of wind. She was not very good at identifying trees. Maybe a cottonwood? She wished her family had gone somewhere during the summer, if only for a short trip, but this year they hadn't gone anywhere at all. She had almost filled her sketchbook. And then she came to the island for four days in a row, and none of her new friends, if you could call them that, were there. She had grown used to them. A little bit of good-natured bantering, a little bit of teasing, a little bit of mock flirtation, the kind you would use on a younger sister. She could tell they didn't take her quite seriously, not like a fellow adult, which was good in a way, because it meant they were protective of her and didn't bother her with untoward attention. She felt safe with them. Not like the guy on the balcony across from their apartment who had stepped on his balcony every morning when she was getting dressed and ready to go to school. Until she noticed and realized she had better lower the blinds. It had left a bad taste. The guys on the island never touched her, not even for a hug. The lack of untoward attention from them was, however, also not a hundred percent good because it left her stranded with her occasional regret that not one of them was about to fall in love with her or try to kiss her or anything like that. Still, all in all, they had given her the romance of living slightly provocatively, if not exactly dangerously, in a summer that was otherwise dull, but productive enough as far as her sketchbook was concerned. A romance of feeling alive without consequence. Now they were perhaps gone for good without so much as saying goodbye.

On the fifth day, however, Jeddy was there, without his guitar, but with the woman Dora. When Willow walked down the steps, they were holding hands, and Willow almost turned around with embarrassment, but then decided to go down anyway. This was her island, too. She nodded to them and walked behind them to the tip of the island, disrupting the three geese that had been grazing there and now dropped into the water, then took off into the air with their loud watery swoosh. Jeddy, usually a cheerful guy, and Dora both looked serious. Willow felt it wasn't proper to look at them, but she really wanted to look, and so she did. Dora was crying. Willow didn't know what to do. She was still standing. They were both sitting on the mossy stones with their feet dangling down toward the water.

"Angelo died," Jeddy said to Willow without looking at her. There was dirt under his fingernails on his hand holding Dora's. Dora's shoulders shook with a sob at his words.

Willow froze. She didn't know how to respond. It wasn't possible. Just last week Angelo had been there playing his guitar. It had to be true, though, otherwise Dora wouldn't be crying like that. Willow didn't want to ask intrusive questions, so she just kept standing, frozen. At first, she couldn't even say she was sorry. She didn't know how.

"It was a motorcycle accident," Jeddy volunteered, now turning his head to look at Willow.

Willow felt betrayed by all the strange emotions welling up in her. She hardly knew Angelo. Or any of them, really. It had nothing to do with her. And because she didn't know Angelo, she really didn't have a right to grieve.

"I am so sorry," she finally managed to say. She didn't want to stay, but she didn't know how to leave gracefully. In short, she didn't know what to do. "I am so sorry," she repeated, scraping her right foot helplessly on the stubbles of grass that remained after the geese had had their way with it. Jeddy didn't volunteer anything about a funeral. Besides, this really had nothing to do with her. And still she felt betrayed. Angelo had no right to die to her knowledge.

I need to go now. Willow wasn't sure she said it out loud. She held Jeddy's hazel eyes for a while. Dora had meanwhile taken her hand out of his and held her face in both her hands, crying quietly. Jeddy's eyes were soft and shining with held back liquid. "I am so sorry," Willow said for the third time and then looked away, quickly scanning the flowing water, some geese bobbing near the riverbank over by the willow. Then she turned and walked back up the stairs, her head filled with a thick, grainy throb, like a protective skin pulled over the beauty of the day. Nothing seemed to penetrate from the outside, not the traffic of the city, not the children chasing each other around indignant street vendors, not the scent of grilled hamburgers and hotdogs. She wished she could cry like Dora, but she had no reason to cry. For her it was all too distant. Something momentous had happened and it didn't belong to her.

She didn't return to the island, though she might return to the upper level to buy that dress she had liked some day when she had enough money, whether she needed it or not. But her first purchase would have to be a new sketchbook. Perhaps she could talk her parents into buying that for her, though, as part of school supplies. School was to start again in just short of two weeks anyway. Everything would return to normal routine. Safe and without surprises. She longed for that sort of unadventurous existence just now. She'd always know what was going to be on the agenda from one day to the next. It was alright. She had wanted to be a rebel, though without tattoos or spiked cuffs, and she apparently had no great talent for even a mild version of rebellion. She didn't crave the cool of danger at all anymore. There was no call to actively pursue it. If it was meant to be, adventure would find her in due course all on its own.

A Child's Voice

I know my name means "man," like Karl or Carl does. Only different.

OK, fine, sure. I'm Karel, I'm eight years old, almost nine actually, and it's sort of good to be alive. Yeah, well, mostly it's good.

I wish everybody could sort out a bit better what's going on. As far as I can tell, everybody is always mad, mad, mad.

I'm just not impressed. It's ugly. Well, sort of. Adults don't make a lot of sense, really. I don't know why. They're always trying to make me make sense, but it's not particularly useful what they do, if you ask me, and so I have a hard time.

It's exhausting. My mom tells me what my shoes cost, and how much my birthday party costs, and my piano lessons. Which I hate in the first place but can't seem to get out of. Sure, I'd love to be a great musician one day. But my piano teacher is ugly. She has a wart on her face, and she smells like garlic and sausage. Plus, I'd rather learn the guitar. Then my mom tells me how much the grocery bills are almost each time she goes shopping, and how much I eat. And what the fees are for voluntary school day trips. So pretty soon I have nothing but dollar signs in front of my eyes, and I'm afraid I'm needing far too much. Then she suddenly says, "Oh, forget about the money. Love is what is important." This usually happens when she comes back from a life coaching seminar, and I'd like to go along because she usually feels good after one of those. But she says I'm too young. Once she took me along for a family night, but that was pretty boring. The other kids were boring, too.

I think my mom really loves me and wants me, but she wants someone else to pay for me. Makes sense, perhaps. She wants that in other ways, too. Like when she goes out with a man, she wants to pick the restaurant, and it always has to be a nice one. But he has to pay. Of course, I'm more important than a restaurant. She says men are providers. Women then decorate the world and make it pleasant. She says one day I will understand that.

See, my mom says my dad's rich, so he should buy party favors for my birthday parties and so on. But then she says he never has any money. And when they were still living together, he sometimes had to borrow some from her, so it's only fair that now he should sometimes have to pay extra for my sneakers or my baseball mitt. So, I don't get it. Is he rich, or isn't he rich?

One time she had my dad over to babysit for me because she had to go some place important. She made us supper first, but she told my dad if he wanted to eat with us, it would cost him ten bucks. He decided not to eat with us but watched us eat, so maybe that day he definitely wasn't rich. It made me feel a little embarrassed to eat, with him just sitting there, and then I got a stomachache anyway.

She really hates him. He once told me he'll always be friends with her, but she says no, they can never be friends because, how can you be friends with someone who has everything he wants when she doesn't have anything that she wants? So, one of them must be lying, except parents don't lie. Maybe Mom does, though, because when I told Dad that she really hates him, she said I'm making it up, and I didn't make it up.

Anyway, my mom says, some lies are OK, so it probably is her lying. But she also says she would never lie to me. But I really don't think my dad would lie to me, either. He's not that kind of dad. So, it gets complicated. When they say opposite things, one of them has to be lying, right? They both always sound so convincing and honest. There's something about adults that I don't get. It probably has to do with the eternal "when you're older, you'll understand" business I get from them all the time. Every time I think I understand something, it gets turned around on its head again.

I've called my mom a liar once, and she slapped me really hard that time and told me never to say that again, and

I never did, though she hits me for other reasons as well. She has to, you know, otherwise I won't grow up properly. Once she slapped me when I called her greedy, too. I was to never call her that again. I won't.

I've called my dad a liar, too. He just said no, he isn't a liar, and when I said, yes, he is, he only said "no" once again. Then he walked away and wouldn't fight about it. So, I guess he's probably the liar, because otherwise he would have defended himself, wouldn't he? Or he would have done something.

But I still love him a lot. And it doesn't feel like he is lying.

They always tell these different stories about everything. My mom says that my dad never came to Germany with us for our summer vacations, although she invited him. But he says he couldn't come because there was always only enough money for one of them to go with me, and, well, since that's where she came from when she was a little girl, she was obviously the one who should go with me, and I have to go because it's part of me, being German, you know. Besides, she knows how to speak the language. He only knows a few words.

I learned that you shouldn't always be too proud of everything that you are, especially when you're part German. They call you Nazi and stuff. The worst was the time I told the other kids that Germans are smarter than anybody in the United States, because that's what my mom said. So, they asked, did that mean she wasn't smart enough to stay in Germany? Wouldn't they keep her there? And that hurt me the most, because she is my mom. I want my mom to be smart, not some dummy who got kicked out of her own country. I think if she had stayed in Germany, my mom would be better than everyone else. Only here in America she has to speak in a different language and so on. It makes it tough. I'm glad I was an American right away. I like English much better than German. German sounds scratchy.

And she is smart. Probably smarter than most Americans. She has taken me on the Lightrail twice now without paying. "If they aren't smart enough to have a functional system for collecting their fare, they deserve being cheated," she said. She saved two dollars and I saved seventy-five cents. Each way!

My mom also taught me that it's no use being proud too much when there's nothing you can get for it. For example, being proud just to be alive, well, that's not so important as being proud of being part of a great school and getting good grades and making the most goals in soccer. My mom says she wants me to get ahead. My dad says he wants me to be happy. Well, my mom says, when you get ahead, then you're automatically happy anyway.

I think my mom has a lot more money than my dad, but she never spends it and so nobody knows. And then my dad always has to give her money so that she can raise me properly. Besides, she really likes money. Especially so we can afford to go to fancy places, like restaurants, and then she has the right to complain when something isn't perfect. "At what I am paying here, I deserve better," is what she likes to say while pointing her nose and looking very fed up.

I wonder why she has to raise me instead of him. Once I heard my dad tell my mom, "Karel is not a business proposition." I'm not quite sure what that means, but I think he might have liked me to be with him then. Sometimes I wish I could be. I mean, what's so special about being a mom? Okay, yeah, so she had me in her body for nine months. I get that. Eight months and twenty-three days actually. But I don't remember any of that. I don't think I was too heavy then. I mean, that's why babies are so small in the first place, so they're not too heavy in their moms. So then what's the big deal?

Was I breastfed? I don't know. I don't think so, otherwise maybe I would remember that. Maybe. But milk isn't so expensive, so it wouldn't have saved too much money to breastfeed me.

My mom's apartment costs over a thousand dollars a month. She tells me that so that I get some sense about what money is worth. I play Monopoly, and there things can cost a whole lot more than that even.

It's hard to not win. But sometimes I do win, because I'm pretty smart. I like playing chess with my dad, too, but I usually don't win then. Only when he lets me, I think. Still, I wish he'd let me win more often. He's had a lot more practice. Mom doesn't like playing chess. I played with her a few times, but she didn't pay attention and she lost, and then she didn't like that. I don't like it either when my mom loses. Usually I like to win everything, but with her not so much, because I can tell that she gets really upset when she loses. And then I get scared.

I like building things. Particularly bridges. Maybe one day I'll become a bridge builder, an engineer. But I also like selling things, so maybe I'll own a store. A toy store would be pretty good, or a store that sells cars, or railroad models. Something like that.

How do I feel right now? I don't know. Sunny, I guess, but with a little bump in there, too. Some tight little bump in my chest where my ribcage ends. I'm not so good at feeling things, and my mom says it's not so important. She feels a lot, but then she has a lot of important things going on. For example the divorce with my dad.

She says it might have been better if my Dad would have just been stronger and stayed with us anyway, but now it really couldn't be helped since he already left.

I guess he must have left my mom because he didn't like her, although at first he did. I think way back when I was very small, he used to love her; he even used to tell her. But then he stopped. Now I think he's afraid of her. More than I am. I know how to handle her, because she loves me. She's too busy loving me to love anyone else ever. She tells me all the time that she loves me, even when she hits me. She does everything she does because of me. Sometimes I like that and sometimes I don't, because then if something she does doesn't turn out so well, then it's my fault.

Anyway, I tried to have them kiss each other, but they both don't want to, especially not deep kissing. My mom likes kissing with me, even deep kissing. It's okay. I don't like it so much. I don't know if my dad deep kisses his girlfriend. My mom says that he does for sure. But how would she know? My mom says my dad's girlfriend is ugly. At first, I thought she was wrong. I thought ugly was different, you know, like really ugly, with warts and a witch voice and farting all the time. Dad's girlfriend isn't anything like that. Still, if my mom says she's ugly—well, my mom knows these things. Besides, it's kind of funny laughing with my mom about how ugly my dad's girlfriend is.

I wish my parents would be together—it's more comfortable that way.

My mom says it's not fair because my dad has everything he wants. But he says, it's almost like that, but not quite. He wants everything he has and that is different. I suppose. I don't quite understand. She thinks a lot of things are unfair. When the sun shines on a day when I'm with my dad, and then not when I'm back with her, she thinks that's unfair, too.

My dad says he doesn't want to fight. But then how come they don't agree? He says disagreeing is not the same as fighting. But what is it then? My mom fights. My dad says it's different ways of doing the same thing.

Most of the time I like my mom's way better. She gets what she wants more quickly. My dad doesn't. He feels easier to be with, though. I don't have to be so nervous about doing something wrong all the time. With my mom I always ruin things and I waste her time a lot. I don't mean to. It just happens. I want to be very careful, because you don't want to do something to ruin things for someone you love. And I do love my mom. Only sometimes I hate her because she doesn't let me be my own person. But she says it's better if I learn to be her person first. After all, she's been around a long time, and she knows what's what. I don't. I still have to learn everything first.

I wish life were easier. There are a lot of rules, and that's supposed to make things easier. But it doesn't really. After you follow all the rules, suddenly there's nothing left for yourself.

Sometimes I have to study German, but not always. Why should I, when everybody here speaks English anyway? She likes to talk to me in German in front of my dad. It's our secret language. It's his fault if he doesn't understand it. It's up to him. He could learn it if he really wanted to, but he's too lazy. He could make more of an effort.

After all, my mom learned his language.

She always wants more money. She likes money. She says she'd be a whole lot happier if we lived in a really beautiful place, like he does. Though we did live there at first, but she didn't like it as much as he did which is why he stayed there and we moved away.

She says she doesn't really want to divorce him. The marriage was just so I could be born and be a legitimate person, and now that I am here, there's no point in just splitting apart. That's what she says. Although she also says he's very bad. He says he isn't bad, but she really believes it.

My friend Tommy Kotts says his parents say it's awful when parents separate. He says it with such a worried face. But so long as his parents are keen on staying together for his sake, then everything will be okay. I wish my parents would have done that for me, not just wish it the way my mom does, despite feeling that my dad is so bad.

I also wish I had a lot of money. Then I would give it all to my mom, because that would make her really happy. I could go to a garage sale and get things cheaply, or even for free. Sometimes at the end of the day, they give you some of their things for free. Then I could sell those for forty dollars to somebody else, and then I'd be rich. Maybe I could give my mom a diamond for Mother's Day instead of flowers. I don't think flowers are good enough for her. She threw them in the garbage once. They still looked very good. Maybe it was because my dad paid for them. If I had a lot of money, I'd give most of it to my mom. Maybe I'd give a little bit to my dad, too, just because I love him too, but he doesn't really want any, or not so much, because he's already happy anyway.

The Boys' Future

The event took approximately two minutes.

Not much later, Gertie Metter clutched at her chest. Silent outrage smouldered in her. To be turned away at the principal's office with a cheesy "We'll take it from here, Miss Metter." She was only trying to help and stand up for the girls. She knew what they called her behind her back: Miss Meddler. Somebody had to do the right thing. Her back ached.

She'd found the girls on the sidewalk just where a trodden shortcut path led into the park on the east side of the school. Kylie was sobbing. Connie had her arm around her smaller friend. "It's okay. It's going to be okay. They slapped my butt too." "But yours wasn't naked." The words came from Kylie's mouth in a vehement blubber.

The gist of their story was that the two girls had been in the park for recess. To save time, Kylie had slipped into the bushes with Connie standing guard so she could do her business. Two boys, Ryan and Johnny, had snuck up on Kylie from behind without Connie noticing. "Show us. We wanna see. Come on, show us." Kylie, mortified, couldn't pull up her panties in mid pee, or in any event opted not to. Both boys had slapped her still naked butt, and once Connie had turned on them, they had taunted her. "You want some too?" They slapped her butt as well, then laughed and took off at a jog.

Even if she was only a part-time substitute teacher, Gertie Metter felt it was her job to do something. It hadn't been on school property, true, but it was still relevant to the school. She could well imagine Kylie's humiliation each time she would have to face the two older boys in the hallway. It was a disgrace. The boys ought to be expelled.

She had persuaded the two girls to tell the principal. She'd even gone with them for moral support. Unfortunately, it hadn't gone as expected. Now the girls were in the principal's office without her support, and she had been dismissed brusquely. The rage still made her breath come out in puffs. She decided if worse came to worst, she would call the newspaper.

Three days later, in the principal's office once again for the third day in a row, Kylie's head felt fuzzy, the same kind of feeling as when she was angry or had a test coming up for which she wasn't prepared. Only it felt heavier this time. Nothing to do with her hair either. How she wished her hair were longer so she could hide behind it. The agony that nothing ever happened quickly when you had to deal with the authorities. She was so tired of everything. Mrs. Salmon, the principal, crouched before her, wearing sweet perfume, gardenia. Kylie knew the scent because her older brother's girlfriend, who was very pretty, sometimes wore it.

Mrs. Salmon was also pretty. She taught fourth grade as well as being principal and had been Kylie's favorite teacher. Until now. Kylie didn't want to listen to her, but she had to. Be polite. It made her face feel hot and it probably looked blotchy.

I don't hear you, I don't hear you, I don't hear you. Her blood throbbed.

"Are you listening to me?" Mrs. Salmon asked in her gentle, warm voice, though today there was a sharpish teacherly edge to it.

Slowly Kylie turned her head from one side to the other and back, just once. She didn't want to look into Mrs. Salmon's eyes.

Mrs. Salmon placed her hands on each of Kylie's arms. "Please listen to me now."

"Yes," Kylie whispered. There was a fog humming in her head. It felt yellow.

"Are you embarrassed?" Mrs. Salmon asked.

"Yes." Tears welled in Kylie's eyes.

"Well, you don't need to be. You haven't done anything wrong, have you?"

"No. Not really." Kylie wondered how her best friend Connie was.

"We want to do what's best for everyone, don't we?" Mrs. Salmon said.

Kylie nodded. She felt abandoned. Nobody was on her side, it seemed. Not even Connie perhaps.

"I know the boys embarrassed you and Connie. I know they shouldn't have. But you are okay now, aren't you?"

"Not really. I feel awful. Really embarrassed."

"And that's okay too. Of course, you feel embarrassed. But what do you think could be worse than embarrassment?"

"Taking a test I'm not prepared for? Or dying, I guess? Or being very sick?"

"Let's talk about Ryan for a minute. And Johnny, too. If you press charges.... Do you know what pressing charges means?"

"Telling something bad happened and saying who did it?"

"Yes. And then that goes in their record, and it stays there, sometimes for the rest of their lives. Ryan cried when he heard that this might follow him for the rest of his life. All his life, do you understand? When he's 70 years old, if it gets in his record now, it might still be on his record that he slapped you."

"But he did. And it was horrible."

"Do you want to remember that for all your life?"

"No. But I probably will."

"If Ryan's records say he touched you inappropriately, then you will for sure. It will haunt you. People will discriminate against him. Think about his future for a minute. This could mess it up. And you will feel responsible."

"But he did it." Kylie worried about being haunted and also about fairness.

"Connie feels it wasn't as terrible as she first said, and she would rather not make an official complaint after all."

"It wasn't as terrible for her. She wasn't...behind the bush. Can I talk to her?" Kylie hadn't been allowed to see her friend since the day it happened. She hadn't seen the boys either, though she had seen Ryan's mother outside the principal's office twice, once just as she was called in, and another time before then.

"No, right now you may not talk to Connie. Right now it really all depends on you. I imagine you want to forget about all this as soon as you can. Instead of remembering for the rest of your life how you may have messed up Ryan's future."

It was all about Ryan, Kylie noticed. Not so much about fat Johnny. Which made sense. Handsome Ryan was a bit of a star at school, very popular with all the teachers. And the kids as well. She too had a crush on him. Until three days ago, of course. Now she was mostly worried about the other kids. Would they hate her and call her a tattletale? She'd never been exactly popular. Mostly she'd lived quietly under the radar. Now they would hate her for turning Ryan in. For a moment, she wanted to ask if the boys would at least apologize for what they had done. Then the moment passed, and she decided she would rather not. She was so tired of everything. It was as though the whole world boiled down to this one moment in time. Three days ago, plans to go to Disneyland were the most important thing in the world. Now nothing like that really mattered.

"So, what do you say?" Mrs. Salmon asked. "Shall we make this an official complaint and file a report and maybe even take it to court? Or shall we just let it drop and go on with our lives?"

Kylie felt drained. She thought again how the kids would hate her. Ryan would for sure. Johnny already did anyway. He hated everyone. "I guess it's okay," she whispered. She knew it was what Mrs. Salmon wanted to hear. Mrs. Salmon talked to her a little while longer, but now she really didn't hear a word she said. It all went over her head as vague noises. Then Mrs. Salmon escorted her to her office door and sent her on her way. Kylie's mother stood waiting for her outside. Ryan's anxious-looking mother was still there as well, sitting on the padded bench to the left of the office door. Kylie saw Mrs. Salmon nod to Ryan's mother. Kylie avoided Ryan's mother's eyes and mumbled a barely audible "Hello, Mrs. Westford." She was too busy with her own mind to notice if there was a reply.

Thirty years later, Kylie Williams was a vice president, one of many, at a pharmaceutical company. Her life was respectable enough as it went, though sometimes she felt it was empty, not quite satisfying. She imagined most lives were like that. She had expected more. Back then, she needn't have worried too much about what the other kids in school would think of her. Her family moved a few weeks later. Her father had unexpectedly landed a new job in another town. She had never married and was not currently dating anyone. She found the dating life tedious, as she found so many things in her life. She wondered whether childhood enthusiasm for anything would ever return and, after all this time, somehow doubted it. One day, she hoped, she would passionately fall in love. So far it hadn't happened. At first, she and Connie wrote to each other for a year or two. Then, when there really wasn't much news to share with each other, they gradually slipped into Christmas card mode.

Connie Gordon made her living as a legal secretary, which paid the bills. She had been married three times and remained friends with all her exes, chiefly due to the fact that she hadn't asked any of them for money in the three divorces. She had a gig as a jazz singer in a local restaurant once a week on Tuesdays, which partially satisfied her craving for glamor and beauty. She really wanted to be a star and was hoping one day someone with clout would discover her at the restaurant. Her audience always seemed to like her, especially when she wore her favorite gold lamé dress.

Senator Ryan Westford was one of the younger members in the Senate and proud to have made his way into politics successfully at a relatively young age. His wife, six years older than he, came from a well to do Mayflower descendant family. They had two intelligent and academically successful sons, and though Mrs. Westford would have liked to have had a daughter as well, Ryan was secretly glad that her childbearing days were over without the coveted daughter. Girls always made him uneasy, like creatures from another planet.

Johnny Breck was in the county detention center for the second time. He had also once been in state prison in another state. County jail was relaxed luxury compared with that. He had once almost succeeded in breaking out by making his way out through the roof. Almost, of course, didn't count for much in the end. As far as he was concerned, all the charges ever brought against him were bogus, and pretty much all the stuff he had done to have landed in trouble with the law had also been done by many others in high places who had gotten away with it with the help of excellent attorneys of a caliber that someone in Johnny's economic bracket simply couldn't afford.

Gertie Metter never called the newspaper thirty years back, though she had gone home to put on some makeup just in case. But then she persuaded herself that it would be as damaging for the girls as it would be for the boys. She had long switched from being a substitute teacher to being a fundraiser for charities and was very successful with that. Currently she was contemplating having her stomach stapled, as she had grown uncomfortably large over the years to her own surprise. She'd started life on the skinny side but couldn't now even remember what that had felt like.

Mrs. Salmon, widowed for many years, retired to an assisted living community on the West Coast quite near the ocean. She had her own townhouse type apartment and loved to host her seven grandchildren who in turn loved staying with Grandma even better than going to theme parks or even to Hawai'i. She was proud that in her career she never had to resort to consulting attorneys or calling in law enforcement, though there had been a few close calls. She gave credit to the kids and the sanity of her exemplary community.

Sound bites

Kylie Williams: If we're all so interested in the boys' future, why don't we stop war once and for all?

Mr. Westford Senior: I was ready to pay someone whatever it cost to make this go away.

Senator Westford: No comment.

Mrs. Westford (Junior): He told me, of course. We don't have secrets. I trust him implicitly. Those girls shouldn't have tattled. It was just kid stuff, like putting a frog down a girl's T-shirt.

Johnny Breck: I have nothing to say. Except that it was all bogus. Like my father always said: Don't ever let bitches interfere with your life. I slapped their butt, for fuck's sake. I've, let's say, improved my MO since then. And what do you expect, with all the trauma of authority bullshit I had to go through at the tender age of thirteen?

Gertie Metter: I only wanted to do the right thing.

Mrs. Salmon: I really liked all the kids I got to work with over the years. It was a privilege.

On the Bus

The tall woman at the bus stop looks French somehow, elegant, self-confident. She wears white high heeled strappy sandals, toenails painted bright red. Crow's feet fan out by her dark-rimmed eyes. She would have been tall even without the heels. An animal print dress peaks out under her open white trench coat. The man by her side looks distinguished in his charcoal suit. His hair is black with silver strands. He is even taller than she is. He rubs her back in a circular motion. She looks enthralled. Her head leans against his shoulder. Her mouth is slightly open, expectant. Her eyes are soft with admiration for him. I could look at them forever.

The bus arrives and a stunning black woman with dark pencil skirt and a bright yellow silky blouse stumbles down the two steps with challenging high heels. Once on the ground, regal bearing takes over.

I get on the bus. To my regret, the couple that fascinated me remains behind. At first glance, all seats are taken. Nobody makes eye contact. Instead, I see many purposeful jaws.

The first row of seats perpendicular to the priority seats in the front of the bus is occupied by a young burly man with his legs so wide apart that he occupies both seats, perhaps in a vain effort to count twice. Before me a slight, bent man with only one leg has entered the bus. I expect the young man to move over and offer him one of the seats. Instead, he growls, "Watch that!" when the one-legged man's crutch bumps his shoulder. Two rows further into the bus, a young woman stands up and offers her aisle seat. The one-legged man gladly accepts.

I move to the middle of the bus where the handrails by the exit door offer more support than the overhead straps which I can reach, but only just. Then, to my delight, a young Hispanic man toward the back of the bus stands up unexpectedly to offer me his seat. I am tired after a day at the office. Lately I have come to not expect this much courtesy. True, I grew up in a time and place where able men would automatically offer their seat to any woman, young or old. That was then. These days, men tend to look fixedly ahead. I understand. They are tired too. We all sleep too little and rush around too much to get as much out of each day as we possibly can, and many of us seem to live and work at opposite ends of the city.

Once seated I have the luxury of looking past my window seat neighbor at shop windows. Used CDs, vegetables, books, a thrift store with two white wedding dresses in the window display. The further we get from downtown, the more billboards appear on the side of the road. Perfume. Underwear. A long-haired Jesus with a cozy-looking lamb nestled in his arms. Bob's Live Bait, Signs West, New Mountain Bank and Trust. Hamburgers. A proclamation that cancer cures smoking. How can one not be in love with this motley world?

On the sidewalk at the next bus stop, a squirrel jumps down from a trash bin, carrying off a substantial chunk of French bread.

Something smells bad. For a moment I am afraid it's me. It turns out a man one seat behind me across the aisle is eating a potent sandwich. Red onions are decidedly involved. And, despite long-standing non-smoking policies, there is always a scent of cigarette smoke mixed with traces of alcohol everywhere, imported on people's clothes and skin and lingering in the dusty blue upholstery.

An interesting conversation takes place between two women seated on the right-hand side of the bus, directly in front of the center exit doors. Actually, it's a monologue by one of the women with a heavily sprayed helmet of short hair and a very strident voice, delivered to her younger long-haired blond companion whose reaction I cannot gauge from the back of her head. I try to ignore the strident-voiced monologue as best I can, but I cannot avoid hearing the triumphant phrase "smuggling Bibles into China." Having recently read a news item about a young woman who received a twenty-year prison sentence for smuggling pot into Thailand, I cannot help but wonder what a Christian would get for smuggling Bibles into China. This thought is probably elicited by the two young men sitting across the aisle from me, one of whom is holding forth about opium and marijuana. At least I think this is a man. Very handsome, though with a disconcerting lip ring. Might be a woman, but no breasts, and a reasonably deep voice, so I imagine it is a man. When his mom went off heroin, he reports, she had endless headaches. Then he describes something else as ten times stronger than acid or mushrooms, most like peyote or mescaline, and completely legal. I am skeptical. His companion, decidedly a man, listens respectfully. He is physically striking, sporting a mohawk with black hair on the bottom, bright red on top.

Meanwhile two boys in the back of the bus, no older than ten, gleefully yell "nipples, nipples" over and over. It seems I am the only one turning around to look at them. Well, at least they are getting some of the attention they covet.

Closer to the front of the bus, a woman is agitated on her cell phone. "Didn't I tell you that?... Well, when I was the one working...when you were getting fucked up...."

On this occasion, the bus driver decides to interrupt: "Excuse me, watch your language, please."

Another voice from near the center exit door: "After he explains it, it always makes sense. He should explain it before the exam. The examples he shows in the book are always so simple, but then in the exam, they are always so complicated."

I pull out a book to entertain myself for the remainder of my ride. At this point, the man next to me tells me that he had once done a paper on War and Peace in college. It was a three-volume set, one about the Civil War, one about World War II, but he had never got around to the third volume. I want to hug him but confine myself to a collegial nod.

At the next bus stop, several more people get on,

more than have exited. I watch a tall man massage his back pocket in search of change. A woman follows, with hair so perfect, it must have taken her hours to assemble. Finally, an old man with a cane climbs up into the bus. He is small, coffee skinned. The driver waves off his fare. No one offers him a seat, so I jump up and offer him mine. He moves my way, surprisingly agile and with a mischievous smile on his weathered face.

"No thanks," he said when he reaches me. "Keep your seat. But if you want to do something really useful, you could always give me a blow job."

Stumped for the moment, I sit back down. My skin contracts around me. At the next stop, I get off. Perhaps he'll take my seat after all. The next bus should be along shortly. They run every ten minutes this time of day. I struggle to offset the eerie sense of shame that seems to have enveloped me and doesn't want to let go. I join a large woman in a white T-shirt clinging to her curves on the bench in the shelter. Her eyes are carefully decorated with glitter dust, and she wears a pink hibiscus flower over her left ear. She smokes a cigarette with quick inhalations and considerately exhales away from me.

I try to remember the look of the woman in love I saw at the original bus stop when I started this day's journey home. Her half-open mouth. Her soft adoring eyes. Maybe she'll be on the next bus. Or at least someone like her.

Business as Usual

Mireille died at 1:15 pm last Wednesday. In the hospital. It was expected. It's been expected for seven months. It is still a shock. She never wanted to die in the first place. Most of us don't. She was so brave. I remember how she worried she would lose her job. She really wanted to keep working, to be useful one way or another in this world. Toward the end, she managed to take extravagant weekend trips with her husband on cheap last-minute flight deals. San Diego, Chicago, Orlando, New Orleans. She wanted to go to Rome, but her medical condition made it too risky to fly out of the country, even for a long weekend. She wanted to make as little fuss as possible.

When Mireille was in the hospital those final days, I kept thinking, what would I do if I had only a few months to live? I knew I would paint as much as possible and live near my lover, both of which I planned to do all along anyway. If something happened to prevent him from moving out—his wife has recently discovered a growth in her armpit, and we hope it isn't malignant—I would cash in my retirement funds, pay whatever tax penalties I'd have to pay, and rent an efficiency apartment up north where he lives. Surely, I can find some temp office work up there. I always have. I always will. His wife doesn't treat him well to put it mildly. It's not the worry about her armpit either, because that's fairly new. Whereas the disdainful treatment has been going on for years. She's having some testing done this week. I pray it's nothing to worry about. I wish I could protect him.

Mireille makes me believe in angels—after all, where else would she go? The afternoon she died, I also found out my ex-husband is getting married again later this month. This too was expected. But they're flying to Hawaii for the wedding. Hawaii! And now I can't help obsessing about them. When I first questioned him about her years ago, he told me, oh, it's nothing to worry about, she's like a daughter to me. Of course, I wish them well and all that, but I also wish for myself that I wasn't quite so vulnerable just now. Thinking about Mireille makes me wish we all were just a little more careful with one another. I remember Mireille telling me how much she loved to hear the other secretaries talking and laughing down the hall in their normal world with all its normal business as usual, bosses, boyfriends, husbands, what's for dinner, the children.

Mireille's boss beckons to me. It's time to go. He's giving me a ride to the funeral. Everybody in our large office—a hundred attorneys, over a hundred and fifty support staff—is theoretically given the time off to attend. Most won't go, even though Mireille was very popular. There is so much to do. People rely on them. And, as always, everything happens all at once. There are motions due at the courthouse. Contract revision deadlines. That sort of thing. Mireille would have liked that, everyone just carrying on.

In the elevator down to the garage, the marble walls look shinier to me than I remember. I don't usually pay much attention to them. Mireille's boss too suddenly mentions how worried she was about losing her job because of all the days she kept missing due to chemo and everything. "She'll always have a job with me," he says. His voice is soft.

Beauty and the Beast: At the Law Firm

The difference between a law firm and a fairy tale is this: in the fairy tale, when the last virgin (usually some patriarch's own youngest daughter) is delivered to the beast (often a dragon, but any beast will do), everyone goes into mourning. In a law firm, when the best secretary is forced to work for the Beast after he has alienated everyone else so that he now works in pampered solitude in his corner office on the 27th Floor, everybody secretly rejoices. They can now relax for a while.

One or two might say a prayer for Beauty. Protect her, Lord, from high blood pressure and other distress.

Publicly the Beast is puppy-dog-eye humble, though he is ugly. If you were to confront him, even right after he has brayed like an ass, he would bat his donkey-length eyelashes. Who, me? The one who just received another award for outstanding client service? Besides, it's her job to know what he wants.

Plus: he likes female tears.

Unlike a traditional Beauty, his secretary didn't volunteer to work for him. But 'let him type his own damn pleadings' would be in violation of his negotiated working conditions, whereas Beauty works at will. In any event, in today's fragile economy, it was impossible for her to decline the honor of being deemed the best, the most likely to succeed.

At first, she hoped (as did everybody else) that she might redeem him. It is a matter of pride to be known as one who can handle anything. But lately her eyes are haunted. Will bestness be rewarded? Not likely. Just now there is another freeze on support staff salaries.

At some point, Beauty leaves and comes back in the nick of time. Things went wrong. She went home to visit her family, that's true. But when she returned, he wasn't lying on the ground under some mulberry bush, struggling with his last breath. Instead, he was in full explosive rage. He'd missed her all right. But it was she who limped to her bedroom that night with dark circles under her eyes and fantasies of committing suicide in his office just to make a point.

Wisely she decided to see a psychiatrist instead, on a fraction of the salary of the Beast who could more easily afford it even in today's economy. She cut back on her wardrobe and weekly fresh flowers and skipped a vacation for which she had saved for two years.

She learned that sometimes a beast is just a beast.

Most nights she dons a peacock-colored gown, floor length, and sits at her window and looks out at stars and dreams, even schemes, of a world in which Beasts become princes and Beauty has the power we have come to expect from her.

Cancer

I didn't mean to break his toy trains. They merely fell out of my hands. Okay, I may have thrown one or two cars against the wall to see what would happen. And the water damage on his stamp collection. He's so magnanimous. He forgave me. I don't think he knows what it's like to suffer. Sure, he gets upset, but then it's all water under a bridge and he keeps right on enjoying his life.

Even now. And I sit here dying.

So, he's coming by before flying to Dublin to pick up his ex-wife, who tried to move back there, start a business and all, but it didn't work out for her after all, it appears, and so they are reconciling and he's going to get her. With fanfare.

I've never seen eye to eye with her. She's always been trouble and only takes up his precious time. Not to mention his energy and money. So now he's flying out to bring her "home."

Couldn't wait until I'm dead. I mean, the doctor has given me two months, more or less.

She once told him, you'll have to choose between me and your brother. She probably did it in her new-age way. *I don't want for you to have to choose, but I see no alternative at this point.* She got that right, I thought at the time, and blood is thicker than water.

Two weeks before their wedding I told him I was worried about his marriage. Which he repeated to her. I think I half wanted him to. Oh, did she ever show her claws. Called me up in the middle of the night and ranted and raved. I taped it as a sort of insurance. It's probably still around somewhere. Anyway, they still got married. And? Did it work? Nah. She left with their three-year-old daughter to go back to Ireland where she should have stayed in the first place, but they didn't want her there either, it would seem.

I still remember the look on her face when I made

some kind of comment about his promiscuous inclinations. You don't mind my saying that, do you? I asked. From the look on her face, she did mind. What? So I say the truth? He did like the ladies, before her, and I would imagine after her, too.

So now they're getting back together, and he'll be happy as a clam. Does not have it in him to suffer. Magnanimously stops by at his dying brother's deathbed for a visit before he flies off to see the love of his life. Tarnished, broken, or otherwise.

He's always been happy. He's always had what he wanted. But he hasn't taught me how to do that.

I don't want to die alone.

I don't want to be the only one suffering.

I want to be loved.

What if I took him with me? I still have the gun in the desk drawer. Wheel my chair over to the desk and take him with me. He'd never suspect till it was too late. And what are they going to do to me? Give me a lethal dose? Torture me for the last few weeks—as though my body isn't torture enough?

I hear the door.

"Is that you, Trent?"

The Choice

I wanted her to love me, of course. After all, she was Colin's elegant mother. But my pots were never scrubbed enough, especially not when I was in charge of our efficiency college apartment and far more worried about Dostoevsky than about pots. And, while Colin cussed freely 98% of the time, when she came to visit, he had it under control. I didn't and carelessly let a four-letter word slip once in her presence. Other than that, I was on my best behavior, and still, she wouldn't warm up to me. Though she did sew me a pretty dress for Christmas one year, and I gave her my second set of inherited amber beads. I wonder what became of them.

Finally, one day my sister-in-law explained it to me. It wasn't about pots and pans or four-letter words. It was about the trip we took together before our wedding, my future mother-in-law, my future father-in-law, Colin, my then-fiancé, and I.

It was one of those old-fashioned hotels in Europe where the shared toilet was down the hall, though we did have a sink with cold running water in the room. It was the last room available, and we took it happily. She was the first one all ready for bed, and she chose the bed closest to the door. She was leafing through a magazine while waiting for the rest of us to get ready. My fiancé meanwhile had plunked down on the other double bed by the window. I had just put on my pajamas in a screened corner of the room and had finished brushing my teeth and was ready to get in bed as well. And suddenly I had to make a choice. Which bed? My future father-in-law was wandering around with his own toothbrush in his mouth, looking out of the window. Maybe that should have been my clue. We had not discussed sleeping arrangements. There was a fifty-fifty chance I would get it right. My reasoning was that my future in-laws belonged together, so they should share a bed. Also, Colin and I were going to be married soon anyway, and clearly none of the four of us were going to participate in any passionate activities with everybody else in the same room. So, I lay down next to Colin. A minute later, my future father-in-law lay down next to his wife. We all said goodnight.

It was the wrong choice. She thought I had disrespected her and never forgave me. She never said a word, not to me anyhow. She was always polite. And frosty. All three of them are long gone now. Recently I found a bundle of letters my father-in-law had written to her from the war, in which he joyfully remembered making love with her without benefit of marriage which didn't take place until years later. It made me smile, and I still wish she would have loved me.

Thirtieth Birthday

Dear Daughter,

I saw your pinched lips at church today. It made me want to laugh. And it made me want to cry. Yes, I am one hundred percent human that way. I don't know yet if I will give you this letter before you leave. I do know we will not mention the issue again in person. It is too difficult. We've never talked much, not since you were a fierce and disapproving teenager to your mildly despised and equally disapproving mother.

I remember my own thirtieth birthday, years before you were born. He adored me then. The photo he took of me picking daisies in a field—you can see how much he cherished me. I'm looking at the photo from time to time as I write this. He was fresh home from the war and couldn't get enough of me, my unblemished, soft feminine being after all those months side by side with his comrades. A young woman picking flowers.

I wish you could have had a thirtieth birthday like that, filled with love, daisies, and admiration. For you it is winter instead, and your girlfriend has just broken up with you, thrown you out in fact and left you temporarily homeless, and you are bewildered by the world and came to visit us for comfort. Not that we can provide all that much.

It is evening now, but I can still see your tight lips in church. I can still feel the heat, the pungent smell of anger from you. You didn't even sing any of the hymns. You have such a beautiful clear soprano. You sounded so strong when you declared yesterday how, beginning with today, your thirtieth birthday, you wouldn't go to church anymore. You were an adult now and entitled to self-determination. You have to go, I informed you. It will hurt your father if you don't. When you're in your beloved San Francisco, you can do what you want, but when you visit us and it's a Sunday or a holiday, you are coming to church with us.

I remember how you used to scream at me when you were sixteen. What do you want me to be—a subservient housewife like you? I never did have as many choices as you did. And, in my defense, I did try to give you wings.

I know this hurts you today, obediently trekking to church with us as always. I wish I could take the pain away from you. You're probably convinced I'm choosing him over you. In this big competition for love that we all seem to live in, maybe I am indeed for the moment proclaiming him more important than you.

No, I don't care much for church either. I don't know what you do to endure when you finally sit there in the pew beside us. I go off into a different world, especially when the music happens to be good, when the organist is on her game. I go because church is his life now, his obsession, if you will. And, yes, I do have to live with him day in and day out. I don't have the kind of wings I have tried to give you. Sometimes I wish I could fly along into wide, unfettered skies.

All I am grateful for is that today Pastor Bader didn't go into a diatribe against women, as he regretfully sometimes does. The organist was flawless, as were the white lilies on the altar. Fly, daughter, fly. I wish I could go with you, but what wings I have are weak. I tell myself I go for the music, for the beautiful light in the stained-glass windows.

I could still feel your fury at dinner. It radiated from you like a fever. I know you did it for me, even as we both claim it is all for him. Thank you for that.

See, I have been trained for obedience. I think I have raised you for obedience and rebellion both. That can't be easy, and for that, forgive me. Fly away. For me it's way too late. I am too old, too tired, and besides I am used to him and his autocratic ways. I cannot change now, and neither can he. Besides, I kind of like him.

Cabeceo

A stately woman sat down next to me, gorgeous, silver hair in a crew cut, flowing black skirt, black tunic, and a wine-red scarf. She swept into her chair with a delicious scent of lilacs.

"I'm Katherine," she said in an alto voice.

"I'm Robin. Nice to meet you."

We watched the dancers on the floor perform their intricate footwork and cheek to cheek tango embraces for half a song. "Do they practice *cabeceo* here?" she asked.

"I don't know," I confessed. "I've heard of it. What exactly is it?"

"Oh, the man asks the woman to dance from across the room by raising his eyebrows or with a nod of his head, and she accepts with a small nod of her own. Or, if she doesn't want to dance, she simply looks away. If she accepts, he then comes over to formally invite her. And off they go."

"Ah," I said. "What if you don't have perfect vision and vanity makes you not wear glasses?"

"Then it gets confusing. You might consider contacts. Also, it's best not to sit in front or behind somebody."

She gave me an apologetic look. She happened to sit in front of me at a cafeteria-style table for eight, her chair closest and most convenient to the dance floor.

"And it's best not to sit in a corner or otherwise out of the way. And you must look perky and eager to dance, of course, and preferably not be chatting with your friends." She chuckled in recognition of our obvious sins.

Unfortunately, I'd been taught exactly the opposite. I was to appear fully engaged, laughing with my girlfriends, and totally surprised when a man asked me to dance, astonished out of my busy personal life. Who me? Now? But tango was a different religion, it appeared.

Katherine kept speaking, sinning, eyes sparkling,

like a connoisseur. Which she was, it turned out. She'd been to Buenos Aires. Twice.

"It's to protect the man's ego. It spares him the embarrassment of rejection. It's just a small gesture that stays between him and the woman. If she doesn't want to dance with him, nobody else ever needs to know."

My youngest nephew came to mind, complaining at the zoo recently how human beings had to eat with knife and fork, no matter how complicated it was, while tigers did not. I wanted to claim just such an injustice here. There was no rule, no *codigo*, for protecting the women from having to sit at the edge of the dance floor, unclaimed in full view of all.

But we didn't get into that because just then a tall young blond man asked Katherine to dance. She danced well.

I was now closest to the dance floor, wishing for a law that would protect my exposed ego, or else for an excellent dancer to come ask me to dance.

Behind the Sombrero

The woman in the audience:

It's hot. A little boring. At least the mariachis have a sail shade over them. For us in the audience, there's nothing between us and the sun. On the other hand, we get to wear whatever we want, while they are in their heavy costumes, all seven of them in identical yellow suits with black and gold trim. Tony holds my hand and wears his lime-green T-shirt with a dinosaur over his heart.

The mariachis play well. They are very tight, flawless, and so good at portraying, creating, evoking good times and happiness. I admire that. They all consistently and invitingly smile except when playing the trumpet or singing a particularly sustained note. One of the younger ones discretely wipes his forehead with a white handkerchief when he is resting his trumpet for a few moments. They play with such pride. I envy their pride, their happiness, their enthusiasm, their smiling sincerity.

Two dancers step in front of them. She first, from the right side, holding the ruffled multi-colored striped hem of her red Jalisco dress up high with both hands. She has red flowers in her hair. He, in a white suit and with white sombrero, joins her from the left a moment later. They circle each other, he with his hands behind his back, she using her two hands to make swirling patterns with the hem of her dress.

I do not like the dancers. Though their moves are perfect and they smile, they do not look happy, not like the musicians. It's probably just envy on my part. I'd rather dance myself than stand here in the sun. He is quite handsome and looks arrogant which makes me angry. She is beautiful and probably about ten years older than he is. She looks confident and also slightly disdainful. When the music draws to a close, he puts his left hand on her waist and with his right hand covers both their faces with his large white sombrero. A clever gesture. But I don't believe those two are kissing behind that white sombrero.

The male dancer:

It's hot. My costume smells. So does hers. I'm really a good guy. I don't know why everybody always has to be on my case. *Bueno*. I'm disappointed too. I thought all women loved to dance. But not the one I really want to dance with. Alena. She'd rather I went to school and got some kind of degree. As though managing a souvenir store to earn my keep isn't enough. I happen to love to dance, and I am good at it. I only do it on weekends anymore. Why can't that be enough?

The female dancer:

It's hot and I am sad. Hope is a blossom. Hope is a claw. I've given up hope. Almost anyway. It's because I am getting too old. And, unfortunately, it is all too obvious. I'm still one of the best. I still have that. But what does it matter? He doesn't want to dance with me. The honors I once craved have passed me by. My husband isn't even here. I don't remember the last time he came to watch me. Three years ago? Or four? Something like that. It was such a dream, and now it is melting.

Once upon a time I was in love with that blond boy from Sweden. We practiced his Spanish together. We kissed. Such shy kisses. Now he is back in his cool home country, married. He sends me Christmas cards with photos of his four children. Nothing ever lasts. Soon others will dance in my place.

. The woman in the audience:

"It's hot," I say to Tony, still holding his small hand. "Let's go find Daddy and get some lemonade."

Tony skips beside me as we move away from the mariachi music and the dancers. So much energy. He looks up at me with a gleam of passion in his eyes. Then he turns his head and looks back at the performers once more.

"That's what I want to be!" he says.

"A mariachi?"

"No. A dancer."

And This Is

"And these are some trees that were all golden. The photo doesn't do it justice. It was magical."

I'd been hesitant to accept Elvira's invitation to tea when we met at a dance three nights before. She could sense my reluctance and became vivaciously persuasive. Among other things, she explained, at the dance the music was far too loud to exchange anything except smiles. She would invite a few of her friends as well, so I'd meet some more people in town. When I got to her house, it turned out she'd changed her mind. Other people could wait. This was now all about getting to know me. The thing about the tea was still as advertised, however. She had no coffee. She did have jasmine tea, hibiscus, peppermint, lemon ginger, cinnamon apple, and chamomile. And, yes, she did have Earl Grey somewhere in a tin. When she couldn't find it, I settled for lemon ginger.

Mugs in hands, we embarked on a tour of her house. Two bedrooms, one converted into an office and sewing room, a large combination living and dining room laid out in an L-shape, a large kitchen separated from the dining area by a table-height narrow wall topped by a wooden shelf. A long hallway divided the bedrooms from the living/dining room and kitchen area, with bathrooms on each end of the hallway. Just about every inch of wall space, including in the bathrooms, was covered with photographs.

"And this is Chaco Canyon. It still gives me chills to think of all that's gone before us. And no, it's not a canyon, really. Or maybe it is, but it doesn't look like one. Not my idea of a canyon anyway. Well, it has to be one, or they wouldn't call it a canyon. One of the guides explained it all, but it went over my head. Anyway, I have some better photos on my phone. I haven't printed them yet."

"It reminds me a bit of...."

"Look, here," she interrupted. "Oh, I just loved these

flowers. They're nothing special perhaps, but so beautiful. And this is Fajada Butte. And here, this is a photo of my friend Gary. He gave me some arrowheads he found during an impromptu picnic on the side of some road. I can show them to you later. And this is, oh, wow, this gives me goosebumps. The sun was about to set, and it started raining, and we got this double rainbow."

She spoke in a whisper now and moved one hand toward her gray eyes, then stroked it over her unruly long red wavy hair that made her look like a Celtic princess. She was captivated by her photos and clicked through one after another on her phone. Some of the images were truly stunning.

"Oh, and this is a red-tailed hawk in flight. I have a tail feather somewhere that somebody gave me. Some twenty years ago. Can you imagine? The bird itself is probably long gone. Across the rainbow bridge. If birds do that. I'm not sure. You know, like cats and dogs do. Maybe birds can simply fly off to wherever they are going."

Her gurgled laughter was contagious.

"I think...," I said.

"I have a great print of this one on the wall in the hallway. Over here." She put her phone in the back pocket of her jeans and led me slowly through the length of her hallway, then back, while we admired framed print after print, first on one side, then on the other.

She wanted to top off her hibiscus tea and offered to make another cup of lemon ginger tea for me. I declined.

"And this is basil. Someone from the co-op gave it to me. It's been growing ever since. Doing well, too." She touched the pot of fragrant green leaves on the kitchen windowsill overlooking her small garden. We hadn't looked at her garden yet.

"I am planning on growing...," I said.

"And this is rosemary," she continued. "And that jar is alfalfa sprouts, though they're not very far yet, as you can see."

I nodded. We wandered back to her living room and

sank down in two deep non-matching brown faux leather recliners facing each other at a ninety-degree angle.

"The shawl on the back of your chair? A former teacher gave it to me. She embroidered it herself. Gorgeous, isn't it?"

It was. I got the idea that people were in the habit of giving her things and regretted that I had brought nothing. I should have brought a small gift.

I touched a pair of high heeled silver sandals standing side by side on the small coffee table between us, rhinestones glittering on their straps and heels.

"I have...."

"Oh, these are my favorites. My friend Alan just fixed the heels for me. No charge. If you ever need any shoes fixed. Let me give you his number." She jumped up and started rummaging in the drawer of a slightly dilapidated looking antique cupboard. I pulled my four-color pen out of my purse to write down the number.

"I don't seem to be able to find it," she finally said, turning to me with a shrug of her slender shoulders. "Oh, look at your pen. I used to have one like that when I was a kid. I think mine was pastel colors, though."

"Would you like it?"

"Oh, no, I couldn't."

"Go ahead. I have about a dozen of them at home."

With a smile lighting up her porcelain face, she accepted my pen. I was certain I could find the shoemaker on my own rather than pursuing the issue further there and then. She placed the pen on a shelf by the cupboard. "Oh, and this is one of my favorite crystals. It came to me when I was wandering on Guadalupe Peak. Or El Capitan. I don't remember which. Isn't it gorgeous?" It was. Six inches in diameter, it had a purple core with a white crystal crust surrounding it. It was heavy when she handed it to me to hold.

"But enough about me and my stuff," she said. "I want to get to know you. Tell me something about yourself."

I didn't know what to say. I tentatively opened my

mouth.

"Are you going to like living here?" she asked.

"I think so. I...."

Her wristwatch alarm went off. "Oh, my God," she said. "Time flies. It's my reminder I have to go and meet my accountant in fifteen minutes. This was so much fun. We have to do it again soon. I want to know more about you. Maybe next time."

Old Man, Park, Bus, Spring

I am tired of inadvertent disdain. It flattens my world.

It is spring. Blue flowers have arrived at the creek in a patch of sunlight on the forest floor, peace seems closer than in the moist frost of winter. Periwinkle, I think; definitely not violets. Because of their sudden presence, they evoke a spontaneous "oh."

Can prey ever truly forgive and forget? No, I conclude. Prey can only always run faster. I am so tired of running politely.

War can be subtle. Inconspicuous. Inadvertent. Or so the predator will claim. His effort is always less while the turmoil of civil war filth takes over inside the prey, like a cancer. Unstoppable.

The prey is often smarter than the predator. It has to be that way. She needs discernment to survive. The predator merely pounces, forgets, pounces, doesn't mean to, pounces, has no idea, forgets, sleeps well. Prey tosses and turns and knows.

Later on the bus, moving away, I still picture you, fleshy face, hear you, good-natured European accent, gruff, in a friendly way, the type who wouldn't hurt a fly. Your voice suits your heavy frame.

You leaned on your orange dog turd shovel. Your lower lip stuck out in that appraising, mocking way of jolly good fellows. Jowls at your jaws and a brown wart on the left side below your large mouth. Hooded eyelids lazily covered eyes of periwinkle blue.

You talked about your wife, who in the past had always spoken highly of you. If you wonder where she is, you hissed with disdain, she's at home. Depressed. Admittedly you weren't a good nurse. You'd threatened her: if she didn't shape up, you'd put her into a home. You sounded put out.

You declined my offer of help. You only wanted to

talk and make me stand still, never mind that I was cooling down in early April sweat.

You said she didn't have sex with you anymore.

What? I asked. I hoped I had misheard.

Sex, you repeated, your periwinkle blue eyes defiantly boring into mine. She didn't have sex anymore. But you didn't mind about that, you said, your thick lip protruding again. She slept with the dog in a separate bedroom.

She would have been horrified to hear you. I was horrified. And I shivered in my ice-cold knowledge that you meant no harm, no real disrespect, neither to her, nor to me, a casual female acquaintance jogging in the park, turned casualty by your unnecessary words. Your inadvertent contempt came easily, as yawning or breathing. I've noticed this with other men. How easily it comes.

A sign on the bus that day, black letters on blue background: "More old people die from loneliness than from any other cause. Do something about it." I greedily scanned the ads for other offerings: cell phone plans, cosmetic surgery, real estate agents, M.A.'s in business. Anything to take my mind off. Nothing did.

You can't even call it war when the prey flees and the predator goes home to his beer and his garlic and computer games, and sleeps well that night, cradled in the comfort of having made a pleasant connection that day.

I want to ask for mercy. But if I stand up to point out the difference between respect and inadvertent contempt, I will likely be drowned out by masculine guffaw, jeering instead of cheering. I will be accused of taking things too personally. And so I keep running, turning away from signs of intelligence on the bus.

I've only always wanted to be good. I would love to do something about the creeping loneliness of the world at war with its own sacredness. Instead, I am so worn out by consciousness, I simply keep running, mechanically, away. When I see you in the park, I turn to jog the other way. I try to be unobtrusive about it. I do not want this war. These days of lovely spring, I try to focus on the beauty. Blue flowers on the forest floor.

Sometimes I fear I cannot breathe in the rank air of jolly poison of incurable contempt of men raised slipshod in a careless world.

And then again the unexpected sigh of early blue flowers. Oh.

Janine

I can't get it to work. It doesn't turn on. And now I can't remember what it's called. So I don't want to ask anybody to fix it. They'll just make it a big deal. They label you so quickly. Of course, they do that anyway and I am already helpless. They explained to me my brain is actually shrinking. I don't know about that. I don't care. I'll sit here and write instead. Some of my memories. Until Alyse comes. I think she comes today.

Last night I dreamt of the knight again. He rides, sword drawn, to defend me. My honor. Nobody has ever done that for me. Not even Harry. Nobody. But today it all crumbles again even though the knight is meant to protect me. His face is beautiful, filled with love and devotion, the way Harry never looked at me. Not after the first few weeks when there was still some kind of gratitude. Our marriage was arranged, of course, and I did what I could. The knight is probably from some fairy tale. A sort of Lancelot. Do you know the one thing missing in most fairy tales? Fairness.

I don't want to struggle anymore. There's nothing worth fighting for. And if there is, I suppose I'll just have to summon my beautiful knight.

Memories are fascinating. More so than this silly old room with its round and soft furniture. When I was just a little girl, the other kids at school called me Janine Stringbean. The only problem was, I was fat. They thought it was funny. I didn't. The trick I learned was to laugh first. My laughter became shrill. My voice became strident. Then they laughed with me, not at me. For a while I even thought I was popular. Truth is, I don't think I ever was. I had funky opinions and made tactless remarks, and everybody laughed. I was never brilliant, but I was funny. They didn't like me any better for it, though.

At home it was the same. Laughter. And when I laughed first, it wasn't so bad.

The other trick was to get sick. Then I got to be important. Even more so than just the personal importance you automatically get when you're a child. I tried faking it when I was tired of all the laughter, all that effort. The trouble with faking it, I always ended up feeling so guilty that I actually did get sick. Every time. My body cooperated by protecting my integrity. Being sick wasn't all that great. I remember some ancient story. Chinese, I think. There was a prophecy that a great flood would come as soon as the eyes of a stone lion turned red. Which of course wasn't going to happen. Everyone felt smug and safe. But then some children decided as a prank to paint the eyes of the lion red. And the flood came. The prophecy had counted on those children. I feel a bit like that, conjuring up forces I don't quite understand.

All that laughter I tried to use to my advantage—and everybody still mocked me behind my back anyway. I lost a lot of weight, but I never did become a string bean. I'm not tall, four feet eight inches, so I'm still pudgy. They were always the nicest people, with little pink guest soaps in their bathrooms, and matching finger towels, matching dishes, linen napkins, polished silverware. And when I talked, people would roll their eyes behind my back, and you could tell they were confident I didn't notice. The way we think things go over children's heads as well, and they never do. Even Alyse rolled her eyes. Everybody knows when there is disrespect. You can always feel it. You become a sort of Edith Bunker, except in my case with a Roman nose. It isn't funny, though you try to laugh with them.

When I fell and broke my hip, it all changed. Now I was respectably important again. I liked that part. But the drugs messed with my mind. Still do, I think, though they are different drugs now. What's good is that now everybody looks at me with respectful sadness, which is almost like a caress. There is dignity in being taken seriously. Though I hate it when my hands get nervous and start tapping or scrabbling on the table of their own volition. Even when everybody is so much nicer, and nobody laughs anymore.

Harry doesn't come visit. I don't know why. I remember how he once said, "Don't listen to her. She's just my wife."

But Alyse comes.

They won't let me have a cat here because cat food stinks. Alyse took the two cats we had. I wish I could hold them for a while.

There's a beautiful young woman in the room now. Alyse? I'm not sure. I didn't hear her knock. She makes me think of that thing in the sky.

"Let me finish my sentence," I said to her to give me some time to figure it out. She smiled. And now I remember what that thing I couldn't remember earlier is called. TV. Television. I merely wanted a vacation from reality and responsibility. And from mockery. Tragedy is much better in that way. I like the softness that comes into their eyes. My thoughts are leap-frogging. I will never tell that it's a trick. Besides, once you start sliding one direction, it's hard to get back. It is pleasant to get smiles instead of laughter. Win some lose some.

I'll simply say to her, "Hello, my dear." That should cover it.

Gray

When Dennis didn't come home from the war, I did the traditional thing carried over from our European heritage. I wore black for a year. Much later I learned the year of mourning was most likely to reassure potential subsequent suitors that one wasn't pregnant with someone else's sperm. Anyway, black looked good on me with my long curly red hair and my delicate ivory complexion. There are experts who say redheads with my kind of complexion should never wear black. They are plain wrong. I looked stunning and I knew it, though it did get a bit boring, especially considering that I was a seamstress. That's how I supported myself and the kids, and I was constantly making beautiful dresses for other women. I wasn't half bad as a businesswoman. My creations were quite in demand, and I made ends meet. I loved working with beautiful fabrics too. Still do. Especially silk. Especially exotic colors and patterns.

When the year of mourning was over, I started wearing colors again. And people started gossiping that I was just trying to catch another man. Looking back, I'd have to say, "just" was somewhat of an understatement. I most definitely was looking. Who wants to go through life all alone? When there are all these fairy tales out there about romantic love and all that? Not that I had a lot of experience with romantic love. Dennis was gone most of our married life, even before he didn't come back permanently. It was always just me and the kids. We did our best.

The truth is always difficult to swallow, though. When I heard Mrs. Kaminski say out loud that thing about me wanting to catch another man, I wanted to strangle her. Lucky for her, I didn't. In my gut, it burned like fire. For weeks. Truth or not, it made it all sound so sordid, so meretricious. I wanted my life clean and elegant. And proud.

I remember too sitting on that bench by the river to have my lunch sandwich when the kids were still in school.

I loved watching the ducks and the ducklings in the spring. It was my treat, time to myself, to dream, to fantasize. I was almost young still, and I was almost happy sitting there by the water with no other responsibilities than watching the light on the water and the ducks in the light. For a while a man about my age, maybe a little younger, came to join me every day on lunch break from his office. He was an accountant in one of the three big law firms. Jeremy, nickname Jemmy. Good looking. Very suave and flattering. Soon enough we started bringing small treats for each other. I started looking forward to his company. He told me he wanted to write a novel.

I remember one fine day we were sitting there side by side, close enough for me to feel his breath. I was waiting for his kiss. All my nerve ending were on high alert.

"I have a wife," he told me. Was it a warning? An excuse? A simple statement of fact? I never went back to the river to find out.

I don't even know if it was him or Mrs. Kaminski's catty comment, but I put my new colorful dresses back in the closet, next to the black ones. Oh, did I mention? I was critiqued once or twice for wearing black, too. It was so dramatic. From time to time when I was alone in the house, I'd put on my lovely and dramatic garments and admire myself in front of the full-length mirror in the sewing room. I know I'm not the only one doing that sort of thing. One time I went into a consignment shop on Main Street just to look at their stuff. Beautiful gowns and skirts and exotic tunics. I asked the young woman managing the store: "And do you ever after hours come and try on all these delightful clothes?" "Oh, yes," she said, grinning from ear to ear.

Anyway, in public I wore gray from then on. On occasion brown or a muted dark blue, and for extravagance an understated silk scarf. They all managed to look better than expected with my formerly red hair, and they still do with my now white hair. But basically, I'm now your generic old woman dressed in gray and wondering why we place all these restrictions on ourselves and on each other. At least I don't follow every cliché for an old woman. I don't, for example, cackle.

Oh, and I never did catch another man.

I am currently sewing a prom dress for my granddaughter. Light blue organza with tiny machine-embroidered white flowers. Sylvia will be so beautiful in it. She already is beautiful anyway, even in her perpetual jeans. I remember one time I offered to buy her a new flutter wrap when the red thing she'd been wearing day in and day out for what must have been years was frayed at the bottom and I simply couldn't stand it any longer. "It's supposed to look like that," she told me proudly. I hope pride doesn't close doors for her as it did for me. In any event, she did authorize the beautiful prom dress I am making for her. In the end, I think we all dream of being beautiful. I only hope I haven't influenced her too much by osmosis with my stubborn pride. I miss the life I didn't live.

A Golden Window: The View from Inside

She sits by her window, a candle lit beside her, as junipers and pinons and the birdbath fade into dusk. Later she will switch on her desk lamp. Often, she sits like this way into the night, reading, thinking, surfing the internet.

When she was a very young woman, she walked past windows just like this one with her schoolbooks in her shoulder bag, and she would be drawn to the soft-gold mystery inside, especially at dusk, especially when mist rose from the river and brisk early winter made her own breath visible. The golden glow of promise seeped into the air to enchant her like an aching dream. The light was so soft, surely those on the inside had to be happy to belong there, women and men caressing, cooking dinner, children with dolls and toy trains or leaning against their mother's hip, later saying bedside prayers, small voices calling to each other, cats rubbing against legs. She wanted to touch those worlds, to be inside them somehow, but her place was always out in the mist, on the outside of the glow, hurrying forward into her future, stopping for just a moment.

Today, if a young woman like that walked by her window, she too might yearn toward its captivating square of gold, a solid world behind it somewhere, drawing attention.

She is safely inside the gold now, dreaming back across the ribbons of her life. A husband, a child long grown and on his own, some music, some adventures, walking across favorite bridges, back and forth, many times. Paris once. She has done well for herself. And yet, the three big ones have always somehow eluded her. Money. Sex. God.

Okay, admittedly, there was always some money. Enough to get by, be fed, be sheltered. Enough for that one trip to Paris. Enough to pay for a friend's lunch from time to time. Enough to wear her favorite clothes until threadbare. But not enough to build the artist's retreat center she had once hoped to create. And not enough to visit her favorite waterfall or to dance tango in Buenos Aires.

And, yes, there had always been a little bit of sex as well. Otherwise, there would not have been her beautiful son, now roaming and romancing the tantalizing world on his own terms. Otherwise, she would not have held on to her husband who was now reading something or other elsewhere in the house. But sex had never really belonged to her. Somehow, it had always made her feel like a stranger to herself, doing her best with an assignment she knew she couldn't ever ace, a faceless receptacle for male satisfaction. She remembers reading early on, with mild pity, about women who could never climax, and still, they claimed, it was pleasant enough, though nothing spectacular. And here she had become one of their ranks. Sometimes she wondered: Was she expecting too much? More than there was or could ever be? Sex had been promised in such shimmering shades, and then society delivered it with its sordid wrappings of contempt. It was hard to own up to the truth of all that, even to herself. Life had equipped her with desire. Her culture had transposed it into scorn and insults. She never got over that. With all her intelligence, she hadn't been able to cross the bridge to ecstasy. A pity, yes.

And it was the same with God. There was always a little bit of God everywhere. God hovered just in the periphery, in flowers, in rain squalls, in all that beautiful wind in juniper branches, in ocean waves and all the invisible stirrings of the nights. How she used to yearn for being one of God's enraptured children. How she was instead repulsed by so much harsh ugliness committed in God's name. A fervent friend once told her: *when you find God, you'll know.* She was still looking. Furtively. Perhaps she was simply not chosen due to endless faults of her own. Though surely the God who had created her would not have simply created her in vain, a rough draft, languishing in the waste basket of the universe?

And so, the hours of gold in her window progress with gratitude and melancholy contentment, with her safely inside. It is exquisite here. She remembers a time only a few years back when she had a crush on a young man who often passed her on a mountain path in those days. She saw him again on the trail yesterday. He looked older. They exchanged a few words.

She: *Finally, summer is almost here.*
He: *I still have to build a fire at night.*
She likes to think of him building a fire.

Acknowledgments

Many thanks to the literary magazines where the following
stories, or versions thereof, appeared:

Bright Flash Literary Review: "Here on the Balcony,"
        "Thirtieth Birthday," and "A Golden Window: The
        View from Inside"
CafeLit: "Summer Music" and "The Dollhouse"
Connotation Press: "Dear Connor"
Constellations: A Journal of Poetry and Fiction: "Surprise
        Visit" and "Lovers or Not"
Crannóg: "I Didn't Know What to Say," "The Mistress,"
        and "Lucille"
Desert Exposure: "Behind the Sombrero"
Eclectica Magazine: "My Brother's Bride" and "Yearning
        Curve"
Evening Street Review: "Not from the Neighbors"
The Feminine Collective: "Two Minutes"
Freshwater Literary Journal: "Unnecessary Mountain," "A
        Walk by the Ocean," and "Gray"
Loch Raven Review: "The System" and "Summer Days"
Main Street Rag: "Janine"
The Ocotillo Review: "Miniskirt"
Olentangy Review: "A Child's Voice"
Otherwise Engaged: "Business as Usual"
Pacifica Literary Review: "Hers"
Piker Press: "The Choice" and "Something Important"
Potato Soup Journal: "Memorable"
Poydras Review: "Conspiracy Theory"
Pure Slush: "Cornflowers," "*Cabeceo*," "Beauty and the
        Beast: At the Law Firm," and "The Wedding"
The Ravens Perch: "Echoes of a Summer," "Love in the
        Afternoon," and "A Liar"
Scissors & Spackle: "Old Man, Park, Bus, Winter, Spring,"
        "The Photograph," and "The Anniversary"
Setu: "The Answer," "Under the Bridge: A Letter Home,"
        and "Mark and Martina"

Short Beasts: "Two Roman Soldiers"
Stirring: A Literary Collection: "Dear John" and "Mardi
      Gras"
Thrice Fiction: "Honeymoon"
Treehouse Arts: "Lee's Story"
The Write Place at the Write Time: "The Gift"

*

The cover portraits of a man and a woman from the late
15th century are commonly credited to the Maestro delle
Storie del Pane.

Beate Sigriddaughter, www.sigriddaughter.net, grew up in Nürnberg, Germany, and now lives and writes in Silver City, New Mexico (Land of Enchantment), where she has served as poet laureate.

www.ingramcontent.com/pod-product-compliance
Lightning Source LLC
Chambersburg PA
CBHW051540050726
47595CB00002B/579